Adolphus F. Warburton

## Loyal Meeting of the People of New-York

to support the government, prosecute the war, and maintain the union,

held at the Cooper Institute, Friday evening, March 6, 1863

Adolphus F. Warburton

**Loyal Meeting of the People of New-York**
*to support the government, prosecute the war, and maintain the union, held at the Cooper Institute, Friday evening, March 6, 1863*

ISBN/EAN: 9783337367824

Printed in Europe, USA, Canada, Australia, Japan

Cover: Foto ©Andreas Hilbeck / pixelio.de

More available books at **www.hansebooks.com**

# LOYAL MEETING

OF THE

# PEOPLE OF NEW-YORK,

TO

## SUPPORT THE GOVERNMENT,

PROSECUTE THE WAR,

AND

# MAINTAIN THE UNION,

HELD AT

## THE COOPER INSTITUTE,

FRIDAY EVENING, MARCH 6, 1863.

---

[Reported by A. F. WARBURTON, Stenographer, 117 Nassau St.]

---

NEW-YORK:
GEORGE F. NESBITT & CO., PRINTERS AND STATIONERS,
CORNER OF PEARL AND PINE STREETS.

1863.

# THE CALL.

NEW-YORK, *March* 4, 1863.

A public meeting of loyal citizens, in favor of sustaining the Government in its efforts to suppress the rebellion, will be held at the Cooper Institute, on Friday, the 6th inst., at 8 o'clock P. M.

Every citizen who is loyal to the Union and the Constitution, determined to preserve the integrity of the national laws and national territory, and to maintain the honor of the national flag, is invited to be present.

General WINFIELD SCOTT, U. S. Army, gives his hearty support to the objects of the meeting, and will preside if his health permits.

The following eminent speakers, among others, have been invited to address the meeting:—

| | |
|---|---|
| HON. GEORGE BANCROFT, | HON. HENRY WINTER DAVIS, |
| HON. JOSEPH HOLT, | HON. JOHN VAN BUREN, |
| GEN. BENJ. F. BUTLER, | DAVID DUDLEY FIELD. ESQ., |
| HON. JAMES T. BRADY, | HON. EDWARDS PIERREPONT, |
| DOCTOR R. D. HITCHCOCK, | HON. HENRY J. RAYMOND, |
| HON. CHARLES P. DALY, | CHARLES A. DANA. ESQ. |

### COMMITTEE ON INVITATIONS.

| | |
|---|---|
| GEORGE OPDYKE, | F. S. WINSTON, |
| JONATHAN STURGES, | WM. V. BRADY, |
| MORRIS KETCHUM, | E. E. MORGAN, |
| BENJAMIN R. WINTHROP, | O. D. F. GRANT, |
| DENNING DUER, | EZRA NYE. |

By order of Committee of Arrangements,

ROBT. H. McCURDY, *Chairman.*

In response to the preceding call, the largest and most enthusi-astic war meeting ever held in this city, since the memorable open air gathering at Union Square in 1861, took place at the Cooper Institute on the evening of March 6th. The meeting was called for eight o'clock, but long before seven the large hall of the Insti-tute was besieged on every side by citizens of every rank and condition in life. To say that the building was crowded to reple-tion is to convey a very inadequate idea of the countless numbers that were packed within its walls. Such unity of feeling, and warm, outspoken enthusiasm for the vigorous prosecution of the war against the rebellion, have rarely been seen at any loyal and patriotic gathering. The army of men which filled the surround-ing squares attested the loyalty of the heart of the Union. The expectation that Lieutenant-General Scott was to preside, was an additional stimulus to the patriotic ardor of the meeting, and every new accession of a distinguished citizen to the platform drew forth loud applause.

The platform was patriotically decorated with the American bunting, and the desk for the speakers was appropriately draped with the same beautiful emblem. Perfect order and decorum was kept, though impatience for the commencement of the evening's work induced frequent calls for " Butler," " Brady," " Van Buren," and other favorites of the people.

At about fifteen minutes before eight, Gen. PROSPER M. WET-MORE descried the venerable Gen. SWIFT in the audience, and insisted on his getting upon the platform, when the audience gave the old hero a rousing cheer, and Gen. WETMORE, ever ready upon an emergency, taking the veteran by the arm, advanced to the front of the platform and said :

" *Fellow-Citizens*,—You do well to cheer this veteran soldier, and will again do so when I tell you that he is our friend Gen. SWIFT, who fought for his country over fifty years ago, and who is here to-night to testify by his presence his devotion to the dear old flag, and his still fervent love for the honor of his country."

Three vociferous cheers followed this announcement, which Gen. SWIFT acknowledged quietly, and took his seat near the desk.

Gen. WETMORE said that there was another gallant soldier present, whom he was greatly pleased to introduce to the meeting. He alluded to Major-General COUCH, commanding the Second *corps d'armée*, now at Fredericksburg.

Gen. COUCH, on coming forward, was received with a perfect storm of enthusiasm. Men and women rose up and cheered lustily for that gallant soldier. The General has a very fine military appearance; his countenance is frank and open, and his forehead broad and prominent. He was simply dressed in a fatigue uniform, and bowed his thanks to the immense audience that so warmly greeted him.

Gen. WETMORE said he had always been satisfied that New-York was true to the Union; but he was now more than ever rejoiced to see that there were so many loyal men whose hearts were devoted to the preservation of the Union and the Constitution.

The next attraction for the audience was the introduction by Gen. WETMORE of the young American drummer boy of Fredericksburg. The General said he had another soldier to present to the audience. The army was not made up altogether of major-generals and colonels. At the battle of Fredericksburg—that glorious battle, though not a victory—one hundred brave men volunteered to cross the river in the face of the enemy, and to spike their guns. This boy—[cheers]—insisted on going with them, but they said he was too small. Nevertheless, he hung on by the stern of their boat, and went over in the water. [Applause, and cries of "What is his name?"]

GEN. WETMORE.—His name is ROBERT HENRY HENDERSCHOT— and he shot a rebel, *too*. He is a member of the Eighth Michigan regiment. This drum was presented to him for gallant conduct, and he will now give you a tune on it. [Loud and enthusiastic applause.]

Young HENDERSCHOT, a ruddy and spirited boy of some sixteen years, came to the front with his drum, blushing deeply as he was repeatedly cheered. With singular facility he played several military calls on his new and splendid drum, and retired amid tremendous applause.

A large number of copies of the speech of Senator FUNK was distributed to the crowd.

The invited guests were the following gentlemen :—

THE PRESIDENT,
SECRETARY OF STATE,
SECRETARY OF THE TREASURY,
SECRETARY OF WAR,
SECRETARY OF THE NAVY,
SECRETARY OF THE INTERIOR,
POSTMASTER-GENERAL,
ATTORNEY-GENERAL,
Maj.-Gen. WOOL, U. S. A.,
Maj.-Gen. McCLELLAN, U. S. A.,
Maj.-Gen. FREMONT, U. S. A.,
Maj.-Gen. DIX, U. S. A.,
Maj.-Gen. McDOWELL, U. S. A.,
Maj.-Gen. BURNSIDE, U. S. A.,
Maj.-Gen. B. F. BUTLER, U. S. A.,
Maj.-Gen. ROSSEAU, U. S. A.,
Maj.-Gen. COUCH, U. S. A.,
Maj.-Gen. SIGEL, U. S. A.,
Brig.-Gen. HARVEY BROWN, U. S. A.,
Brig.-Gen. J. G. BARNARD, U. S. A.,
Brig.-Gen. JAS. S. WADSWORTH, U. S. A.,
Brig. Gen. COCHRANE, U. S. A.,
Brig.-Gen. CORCORAN, U. S. A.,
Brig.-Gen. F. P. BLAIR, U. S. A,
Admiral GREGORY, U. S. N.,
Admiral STRINGHAM, U. S. N.,
Admiral PAULDING, U. S. N.,
Gov. SEYMOUR, of New-York,
Gov. ANDREW, of Mass.,
Gov. BUCKINGHAM, of Ct.,
Gov. CURTIN, of Pa.,
Gov. SPRAGUE, of R. I.,

Gov. ANDREW JOHNSON, of Tenn.,
Hon. IRA HARRIS,
Hon. PRESTON KING,
Hon. E. D. MORGAN,
Hon. WM. PITT FESSENDEN, of Me.,
Hon. J. B. HENDERSON, of Mo.,
Hon. D. K. CARTER, of Ohio,
Hon. H. WINTER DAVIS, of Md.,
Hon. JOSEPH HOLT, D. C.,
Hon. JAMES A. WRIGHT, of Ind.,
Hon. GEORGE BANCROFT,
Hon. JAMES T. BRADY,
FRANCIS HALL,
Hon. HENRY J. RAYMOND,
WILLIAM CULLEN BRYANT, Esq.,
Hon. CHAS. P. DALY,
HORACE GREELEY, Esq.,
JAMES GORDON BENNETT, Esq.,
Hon. JOHN VAN BUREN,
R. D. HITCHCOCK, D. D.,
GARDINER SPRING, D. D.,
WM. B. MACLAY, Esq.,
DAVID DUDLEY FIELD, Esq.,
Hon. MOSES F. ODELL,
Hon. JAMES WADSWORTH,
PRESIDENT AND MEMBERS BOARD OF ALDERMEN,
PRESIDENT AND MEMBERS BOARD OF COUNCILMEN,
PRESIDENT AND MEMBERS BOARD OF SUPERVISORS.

At eight o'clock precisely, Gen. WETMORE said :—

" *Gentlemen*,—It is my privilege to call this meeting to order. Gen. SCOTT will not be with you to-night. Yesterday morning, he was well enough to enter into an engagement with me to call for him this evening. I saw him again this morning, and he was still well enough to justify confident hopes of his presence. At 7½ o'clock I found him in bed, suffering from a severe attack of incipient pleurisy, and his physician had peremptorily forbidden his going out of his room. He desired me to express to this meeting his great regret at the necessity for his absence, and his cordial assurance that he is with you earnestly and heartily in your movement in favor of the loyal cause. [Cheering.] No man could use stronger terms than did that distinguished patriot, soldier and citizen, in the assurances he gave me of his desire to be here to-night. In his absence, it would be my duty to nominate as your presiding officer, His Honor the Mayor. [Loud cheers.] Punctual, prompt, and attentive as he always is, some great necessity must have detained him ; and I am at this moment assured that so great is the crowd outside that it is impossible to penetrate it. In his absence, I now present to you for your presiding officer, temporarily or permanently, WILLIAM CULLEN BRYANT." [Enthusiastic applause.]

Mr. BRYANT said :—" *Fellow-citizens*,—I am called on very unexpectedly, absolutely unexpectedly, to preside over this meeting. I rejoice to see so many of my fellow-citizens here present. It is a proof that they are animated by a loyalty that is beyond all danger from qualification, or dilution. Gentlemen, you will excuse me from addressing you at any length this evening, while there are so many eloquent speakers ready to utter what I am sure must be in all your hearts—sentiments of devoted fidelity to the Union and the Constitution. [Cheers.] I will call upon the Rev. Dr. HITCHCOCK, who will now address you." [Cheering.]

### SPEECH OF REV. DR. HITCHCOCK.

FELLOW-CITIZENS OF NEW-YORK,— Fellow-citizens of our once and our still glorious Union, [applause,] I did not feel quite sure that I should be called upon to say anything this evening. I did not at all expect to be called upon to stand first in your presence. Mr. President, if this is not an uprising of the people, I have never seen an uprising of the people, and to my dying day I never expect to see one, [applause;]—an uprising, in my judgment, more grand, because more solemn and more stern, immeasurably more stern and solemn, than that uprising of April, 1861. [Applause.] When rebel cannon first opened its roar on Sumter, the people started to their feet in a frenzy of patriotic passion. That earliest passion of the people was like heat lightning. [At this point Mayor Opdyke appeared on the platform, and was greeted with applause.] That earliest passion of the people, as I was saying, was heat lightning on the far horizon.

The present passion of the people, which has been fed by the thought and by the sacrifices of months, is chain lightning overhead, and it will rive this rebellion to its base. [Cheers.] What was then an instinct, that this Union must not be dismembered, is now a conviction as deeply rooted in our hearts and as sacred to us as our faith in God. [Applause and cheers.] We regard ourselves as but fulfilling a divine decree.

The shape of the continent itself dictates but a single Government to dominate throughout the continent, from the chain of lakes in the North to the Gulf of Mexico and the Isthmus of Panama in the South. [Cheers.] From those lakes northward, the continent slopes to the pole; from those lakes southward, the continent slopes to the Gulf of Mexico; and although we propose no raid on Mexico, we read the finger of destiny dictating the unity of the continent in its government as in its geography. [Applause.] From those silvery lakes clear down to the Isthmus, there can be but one government. Suppose we consent to these craven counsels which are crying "peace" when the Lord hath said, "There shall be no peace to the wicked." [Applause.] Peace, with dismemberment, for its immediate price, will entail upon us eternal war and final chaos, strewing the continent with the wreck of all that we have valued in our institutions and our hopes. The continent has also been peopled by substantially one race; two thirds of the inhabitants of the present States of our Union are Englishmen, in blood—one third peopling New England, and one third peopling the Southern States—and these furnish the syntax of our history. The other third, Irish, German and all the rest, under the providence of God, have been gradually distilled into our blood, and this grand amalgam we hail as the new American people of history—as the gift of God to this Continent. [Cheers.] These elements are to be welded all together.

A VOICE.—No, we are not Englishmen.

DR. HITCHCOCK.—I heard some one crying out against the English.

A VOICE.—An Irishman, sir. [Cheers and laughter.]

DR. HITCHCOCK. My friend, it was not from the loins of the English aristocracy, which has set its proud heel on your nation's neck that this continent has been peopled, but by the middle- the sturdy middle class of England, whose hearts beat true with ours to the music of the Union. [Applause.] There is another

England making itself heard in Exeter Hall, making itself felt even in the seat and in the centre of power, and the future of England is in the stout hands and in the sturdy loins of that middle class from whom we derive our descent. [Cheers, and cries of "That's so."] We are one people ; we have taken largely of Ireland, and we are thankful for the contribution. [Applause.] The green island will be represented by a silvery tongue which we shall be glad to hear. [Applause, and cheers for Brady.] We are thankful, too, for the honest Teutons who follow Sigel in his career. [Cheers.] These are all no more Englishmen, no more Irishmen, no more Germans, but they themselves bless God that they are Americans. [Cheers.]

We recognize a great diversity of material interests, taking all the States of the Union into the account. We find the Atlantic sea-board, by the decree of Providence, dedicated to commerce and manufactures. We find the great rich Northwest dedicated to corn, which makes strong the heart of man. We find the South dedicated to cotton, sugar and tobacco. These interests are diverse, but in their diversity lies the hiding of a higher unity. These material interests may all combine and co-work to accomplish unity in our political destiny. [Applause.] Why, then, this mad attempt to break this continent, by breaking the back of the Alleghanies, which God has planted as the indication of His will and purpose concerning us ? This chain of mountains has not been wheeled across the continent from East to West, dedicating it to two governments, but up and down the continent, North and South, laying open the continent to the bracing winds of the Arctic and to the soft breezes of the tropics. These mountain ranges, running north and south, have opened the continent to the majestic tread of a single people. [Applause.]

Why, then, are we divided ? The heart of the controversy, when we reach it, is simply this :—A death-duel between Democracy, under whose banner the continent was taken and occupied, and an aristocracy, which is a most grievous anachronism, out of time in this nineteenth century ; out of place on this Democratic continent—[applause and cheers]—an aristocracy which intensely hates every article in the Democratic creed ; an aristocracy which has spit and trampled on the Democratic creed ; an aristocracy which, in the presence of its chief expounders, has declared a final war against Democratic ideas and Democratic institutions. Of what this aristocratic sentiment has been born I need not tell you. The Vice-President of the Southern bastard Confederacy—the great high-priest and chief apostle of this Luciferian revolt—has said :—"The corner-stone of our Confederacy is slavery." Slavery, as black as ebony, as black as night, as black as hell. [Applause.]

The chief objection to the Administration, in its gallant attempt to throttle and utterly put an end to this rebellion, is, that it has proclaimed liberty to the captive. [Prolonged cheers.] I am afraid you are all abolitionists. [Repeated cheering.] What has the Government done in this matter ? It has found this rampant rebellion rushing on the Capital, and striking at the heart of the nation, mounted on black shoulders, and at last it has taken the resolution that this black underpinning shall be knocked out, [applause,] and that the rebellion, on its own honest or dishonest feet, as the case may be, shall meet us foot to foot, and eye to eye, and breast to breast, and then it will be known whether twenty millions of Democratic Republicans, standing on this continent, consecrated to Democratic Republicanism, shall be a match and an overmatch for eight millions of rebels. [Applause.] The Administration has determined that this issue shall be fairly tried. Military necessity, military wisdom, has dictated this measure purely and sheerly; and shall we not bless God for the opportunity which he has given us to compass a magnificent achievement of holy justice in the name and under the wavings of our starry flag? [Applause.]

We strike for our institutions, for the graves of our fathers, for the cradles of our children, and we strike that grander blow for humanity, for man as man. [Cheers.] And now, beneath the auspices of these new measures, the voice of the nation, that war choked almost to silence, bowing to the dust, is pealing across the ocean in clarion tones. The heart of the true England is responding to us. Every true Frenchman, every true German, every true Christian man of Europe is on our side. [Applause.] It seems paltry in us to have misgivings in this eleventh hour. The rebellion is almost quelled. The last blow for our institutions is almost struck, and shall we now be false to ourselves in this final trial? By the memory of our fathers, by our hopes for our children, by our faith in God, the Father of all mankind, no, no, a thousand times NO. [Great applause.]

GEN. WETMORE.—His Honor the Mayor having appeared, it is now in order to move the adoption of a list of officers of this meeting. With your permission, Mr. Chairman, I will read the first half dozen, and then I will ask the meeting, under your guidance, to take the rest upon trust, for I can venture to give the assurance that there is not the name of a man there who is not loyal to the country. I respectfully nominate for

### Vice-Presidents.

| | | |
|---|---|---|
| GEORGE OPDYKE, | HAMILTON FISH, | WM. B. ASTOR, |
| JOHN A. KING, | PELATIAH PERIT, | LUTHER BRADISH, |
| GEORGE BANCROFT, | F. B. CUTTING, | ROYAL PHELPS, |
| A. A. LOW, | JAMES LENOX, | CHAS. H. MARSHALL, |
| ALEX. T. STEWART, | JONATHAN STURGES, | C. R. ROBERT, |
| W. F. HAVEMEYER, | JOHN A. STEVENS, | JOHN D. WOLF, |
| MOSES TAYLOR, | E. PIERREPONT, | G. C. VERPLANCK, |
| BENJ. L. SWAN, | DENNING DUER, | M. O. ROBERTS. |

B. R. Winthrop,
Wm. Whitlock, Jr.,
Morris Ketchum,
Robert L. Stuart,
W. C. Wetmore,
Wm. M. Evarts,
James Boorman,
Samuel E. Low,
Isaac Bell,
Francis Lieber,
Ezra Nye,
George T. Elliott,
James G. King,
George Griswold,
Peter Cooper,
Charles Gould,
S. B. Chittenden,
O. D. F. Grant,
B. H. Hutton,
George T. Adee,
William Barton,
Benj. W. Bonney,
H. W. T. Mali,
Shepard Gandy,
George S. Coe,
Daniel Drew,
Frederic Depeyster,
R. A. Witthaus,
Henry H. Elliott,
E. D. Stanton,
Charles Butler,
George F. Talman,
S. Kauffman,
W. M. Vermilyea,
Joseph Hoxie,
Jas. W. Beekman,
Jas. B. Nicholson,
Benj. H. Field,
Pierre Humbert,
A. C. Kingsland,
George Denison,
Lewis B. Woodruff,
Henry B. Stanton,
Charles B. Spicer,
Michael Ulshoeffer,
George H. Purser,
Townsend Harris,
Joseph Lee,
Cornel. Vanderbilt,
Adam W. Spies,
P. S. Forbes,
S. S. Wyckoff,
Lloyd Aspinwall,
Waldo Hutchins,
A. J. Bleecker,
Marshall Lefferts,
John E. Develin,

John J. Cisco,
C. H. Russell,
John C. Green,
Joseph Lawrence,
Samuel Sloan,
R. H. McCurdy,
F. S. Winston,
Nehemiah Knight,
R. D. Lathrop,
Wm. Curtis Noyes,
W. W. De Forest,
Sam'l Wetmore,
R. L. Kennedy,
S. Cambreleng,
Simeon Draper,
E. E. Morgan,
William Orton,
Geo. F. Nesbitt,
E. Delafield Smith,
Joseph Ripley,
James B. Murray,
Henry E. Davies,
Joseph W. Alsop,
Wm. C. Gilman,
Robert Bayard,
John Jay White,
Hugo Wesendonck,
Wm. T. Coleman,
Jeremiah Burns,
Wm. B. Maclay,
Math. T. Brennan,
Floyd Smith,
Nathaniel Hayden,
Samuel Blatchford,
Rufus F. Andrews,
Chas. W. Sandford,
W. C. H. Waddell,
Ferd. Lawrence,
Abra. R. Van Nest,
George Irving,
James K. Pell,
John Ewen,
Courtland Palmer,
Edward P. Cowles,
A. M. White,
Erastus C. Benedict,
Thos. C. Smith,
Charles Yates,
Thos. C. Acton, *
Samuel Beman,
Wilson G. Hunt,
Leonard W. Jerome,
John A. Lott,
John D. Townsend,
Hawley D. Clapp,
T. G. Churchill,
Wm. A. Darling,

Charles King,
J. J. Phelps,
Shepherd Knapp,
Geo. S. Robbins,
Wm. V. Brady,
J. J. Astor, Jr.,
Wm. G. Lambert,
Wm. E. Dodge,
Moses H. Grinnell,
Henry K. Bogert,
H. G. Stebbins,
James L. White,
Hiram Barney,
John Wadsworth,
Aug. C. Richards,
Geo. Cabot Ward,
Orison Blunt,
And'w Carrigan,
Robert T. Haws,
James Benkard,
Morris Franklin,
Sam'l T. Skidmore,
Abram Wakeman,
E. C. Cowdin,
Cyrus W. Field,
Edwin Hoyt,
Geo. W. Blunt,
D. Van Nostrand,
Seth B. Hunt,
Samuel B. Ruggles,
George T. Strong,
C. Astor Bristed,
George B. Butler,
Wm. F. Blodgett,
B. F. Manierre,
Frank E. Howe,
James R. Whiting,
George Bisbee,
Fred. A. Conkling,
Elijah Fisher,
Jacob A. Westervelt,
John B. Borst,
Wm. Mitchell,
Murray Hoffman,
James F. Depeyster,
Abra. M. Cozzens,
Wm. H. Aspinwall,
John McKesson,
Wm. H. Webb,
Henry A. Heiser,
Henry O. Rielly,
Harvey P. Peet,
John Slosson,
George Law,
Nathl. Jarvis, Jr.,
H. A. Smythe,
Wm. B. Taylor,

William H. Lee.
Horace B. Claflin,
A. Vanderpool,
Charles Anthony,
Geo. H. Moore,
John Slade,
George P. Nelson,
Floyd Bailey,
L. Sherwood,
Sinclair Tousey,
John Chadwick,

Philip Tillinghast,
J. R. Livingston,
Erastus Goodwin,
James Low,
H. Blake,
S. Hutchinson,
Wm. H. Fogg,
Wm. A. Budd,
Jos. W. Patterson,
Alfred G. Benson,
Josiah S. Bennett,

James Kelly,
Wm. H. Mellen,
John H. Almy,
J. A. Pullen,
Charles Roome,
W. Curtis Noyes,
Wm. W. Stone,
S. D. W. Bloodgood,
Luther B. Wyman,
C. E. Detmold,
Benj. C. Thayer.

### Secretaries,

Wm. Allen Butler,
Ed. C. Bogert,
John Austen Stevens, Jr.,
Wm. H. L. Barnes,
John H. Draper,
W. L. Ellsworth,
Ethan Allen,
Andrew Warner,
E. A. Wetmore,
F. G. Swan,

Chas. E. Strong,
Spencer Kirby,
Theodore Tilton,
A. M. Palmer,
N. W. Burtis,
F. W. Ballard,
Wm. S. Opdyke,
John Ordronaux,
John Heckscher,
G. W. Nichols,

Edward King,
Charles H. Ludington,
R. A. McCurdy,
Wm. P. Lee,
Cephas Brainerd,
C. S. Spencer,
Frank Moore,
W. O. Bourne,
Geo. W. Benson,
R. J. Vanderburgh.

When the name of Mr. A. A. Low was announced, Gen. Wetmore said:—"Let us give a fitting reception to the name of the honored merchant who has done so much with his voice, his pen and his purse, for the upholding of our Government, while the flames of his burning property, (alluding to the loss of the *Jacob Bell*,) were lighting the track of Rebel Pirates over the ocean." Whereupon the audience gave three cheers, and Mr. Low acknowledged the same, courteously bowing.

The gentlemen named were unanimously elected.

Mr. Bryant:—"Now, gentlemen, will you allow me to do what was intended should be done in the outset, to resign the seat to which I have been called, to the Mayor of this city, a gentleman who brings to the work of presiding over you more than the dignity of his office, who brings sterling worth, undoubted integrity and sound understanding, and who is worthy to preside over a meeting of loyal citizens like this? I ask, in answer to this, only the enthusiastic acclamation which you are ready to give, and if you will say 'Aye,' say it in thunder tones."

A thundering Aye greeted the proposition, and amid loud applause, His Honor, Mayor OPDYKE, took the chair.

He said :—"I regret exceedingly that my slight delay should have caused any interruption in the opening of this meeting. I had understood that one of our most distinguished citizens, whom we delight to honor, was to preside, and supposed, of course, that I was not to be called upon to officiate. And when I came to find another citizen, whom we equally delight to honor, in the chair, I felt that the place was much better filled than I could fill it. I owe you, however, this apology, and I think it is a good one, for my non-appearance earlier : I left home early enough to be here at eight o'clock, but at the entrance of the hall I was met by a solid mass of patriotism which restrained my movements. [Laughter and applause.] Gentlemen, I will not detain you with any remarks. I cannot, however, resist the temptation to say that the object of this meeting meets my most hearty approval, and it rejoices my heart exceedingly to witness the generous response with which it has been met. Without detaining you further, I have great pleasure in introducing you to those sweet silver tones which represent the Emerald Isle. I have the pleasure of introducing JAMES T. BRADY, Esq." [Cheers.]

### SPEECH OF JAMES T. BRADY.

MR. CHAIRMAN AND FELLOW-CITIZENS OF NEW-YORK,—You have heard the reference to silver tones, as if, indeed, a trumpet of the festival were to be heard when I had the honor and pleasure of addressing you. During the last few minutes I have had serious doubts where I was, in truth, born. [Laughter.] My earliest recollection is, that I derived my nativity in the city of New-York, of which your worthy Chairman is the Chief Executive officer ; but, with the accustomed self-appreciation of the race from which I sprung, I think I may become the competitor of Homer, and have the world divided in opinion as to where I was born. [Laughter.]

A VOICE.—Louder! We can't hear what you say, and we came here to hear you. [Laughter.]

MR. BRADY.—Which to me is a great gratification ; for it is so long since I discovered that anybody wanted to hear what I said on any subject, that my vanity is gratified to the extreme. [Laughter.] I recognize in the voice that first broke silence at this magnificent meeting, those rich tones which he who was to have presided here once declared gave pleasure to his heart, [applause,] and it does not become me, as a descendant of the Green Isle, to admit that there is anything less than music in anything that comes from that source.

I am a little disappointed, however, because I expected to have the pleasure and instruction which every man, however great he may be in intellect, capacity, or merit, will undoubtedly receive, if he be American born or American in heart, in the privilege of looking upon a form that was to have been here to-night. [Applause.] All of you remember that Washington Irving, in his beautiful essay upon Stratford-on-Avon, said it was something to have seen the dust of Shakespeare But it is more than that to find the genius of the American people at this hour expressed in the two words that form the name of Winfield Scott. [Applause.] He is absent from this procession to-night. I call it a procession, although you sit here stationary, because it is a movement to a result which no physical power can thwart. [Loud applause.] Cato's statue is indeed absent, but Cato lives, thank God, and will live for years. I am also disappointed in not hearing the clarion tones of that great son of Kentucky whose loyalty is equal to his eloquence, and that is the highest compliment I can pay him—Joseph Holt. [Loud applause.] And yet I should be gratified with this circumstance, because those who hear him, unless he has failed since I last enjoyed that pleasure, wish for no other gratification, when he has spoken. But here I am, with all these deficiencies charged upon myself—a mortal man of the 19th century, with no greater hope than that I may be honored with the position described by your President, [Mr. Bryant,] in that beautiful poem denominated June, which gladdened the inmost recesses of my heart when I first began to love poetry as the synonym of freedom and truth—

" Whose part in all the pomp that fills
The circuit of the Summer hills,
Is that his grave is green."

But I want it to be distinguished as the grave of one whose country was the United States of America. [Loud cheers.] That is my country. I can admit of no other. There is no name to be substituted for that. There is no flag except ours that I can ever accept, [cheers,] no star to be taken out of it, [cheers,] no stripe to be stolen from it, [cheers,] stars to be added to it without number, [cheers,] stripes to be accumulated till the eye tires of looking at them ; so that, with all the gallant history of its past, and glorious associations of its present, however gloomy the prospect may appear to many, there shall be for us, now and hereafter, one country, one constitution, one destiny. [Loud cheers.]

I was dining with a friend to-day, who read to me an extract from a newspaper—The Express, [laughter, and expression of disfavor]—saying that this was a meeting of Abolitionists, and that Brady would not be present. I am not entirely certain that I am, for there is so much of individuality and spiritual power and tendency to great results in this chamber, charged with patriotism, that I am like nothing in this majestic presence. [Applause.]

But, so far as I am capable of knowing myself, I am here—here with delight—here with pride. [Applause.] Although from the first time that I ever made a speech in public till now, most of you have been opposed to me, as I well understand, in the political sentiments that have affected the general question which has determined who should hold the highest offices in the republic, I thank God that it has been permitted me to be present on an occasion when any one human being would attach importance to my voice in saying that I stand up now, as I always have done, for the preservation of the Union and the Constitution of the country. [Loud cheers.] When I began life I heard, as I afterward heard, a word called Yankee. It certainly does not apply to me. But the South has applied that word to all of us at the North. Now I am free to say that I discover in the Yankee character some particular features that I no more admire than I do some of the prominent traits in the inhabitants of the land from which I sprang. But I nevertheless accept the name of Yankee as applied to me in the spirit of our forefathers in the revolutionary period ; and if the South can find no more of disgrace to be attached to it than its undying struggle for the preservation of this Government, whether slavery exists or falls, I thank God for it. [Loud applause.] You will pardon me, my fellow-citizens, if I offend the prejudices of some of you in speaking my mind. The first speech I ever made for a presidential candidate was in behalf of a southern man. From that time to this my sympathies have been strongly with that portion of the Union. But, gentlemen, to make the matter terse and pointed, if I lived in a house with a friend, and he announced to me some day that under no circumstances would he associate with me any longer, I would propose to vindicate what is manly in my nature by telling him that I would go somewhere else where I could find suitable company. [Great merriment and applause.] As I came here to-night, and as I passed through the streets to-day, I was beset by gentlemen for whom I have the greatest respect, who wondered whether I would speak at a meeting where gentlemen always opposed to us in politics would be present, and where perhaps a spirit of freedom stronger than any that had entered into their natures might be exhibited. [Applause.]

Gentlemen, I differ with many of you in regard to the causes, the conduct, the prosecution, and the probable results of the war in which we are engaged. But, with the blessing of Heaven, whoever may applaud and whoever may censure, I would be false to the Irish race, from which I spring, who find here a home and a refuge from the persecution and oppression of that detested land to which the first speaker too politely referred, [applause and a hiss,] if I did not use my last breath, and employ the last quiver of my lips, in the utterance of a prayer to Heaven against all assailants, internal and external, for the preservation of the American Government. [Loud applause.]

When this war broke out, I knew that it was urged on by the South. I hoped that it might terminate early ; I hoped that my Southern countrymen—for such they are—would develop among them some desire to remain with us. I detected with regret that they had prepared means to make an assault upon a Union that they ought to love. I maintained silence in regard to it. You will excuse my egotism, but I now justify myself in my own presence. I found that they proposed to take to themselves Fort Sumter, the forts at Key West and Pensacola, Tortugas and Fortress Monroe. I thought it was quite essential to the dignity and prosperity of the country that we should retain these fortresses. I think so now. I did hope, however, that the Southern people would put their feet upon the necks of their leaders, and insist upon the maintenance of the Union. But they have informed us that they would consent to no such condition. They have told us that if we gave them a blank paper and pencil to write the terms of a new compact, they would not agree to it. Therefore it is a war declared for all ultimate results that can come, and I spit upon the Northern man who takes any position except for the maintenance of the Government. [Here almost the entire audience rose to their feet, waved their hats, and cheered vociferously for some moments.] I surrender here all opinions that may sway a Presidential contest. I surrender all inquiry as to who shall be Governor of any State. I give up all predilection as to who shall be Mayor of the city of New-York—although I have no great objection to my friend, the President of the meeting, for whom I did not vote. [Laughter.] I stand here in the presence of the assembled multitudes of the past. I feel glowing within me what may have animated the heart of the Egyptian, when, chained to one of the great stones that was to form part of the magnificent pyramid to illustrate the majestic powers of the crumbling mortal who was to perish within them, he felt that the time would come when there should be a government of freedom in the world. I have within me the hope of the poor serf in Russia, the enthusiasm of the young Hungarian, who, by the little flickering flame of freedom, even though it be in a dungeon, finds himself stimulated with the hope that he may once see a land beyond the deep, not revealed, perhaps, even to a Moses from Mount Pisgah, where a free people have established a free government. And in the name of Almighty God, I invoke such curses as He may permit, innocuous as mine may be, to put an end to any man who would destroy a structure like that. [Loud applause ] Are there such men ? There are. Let me allude to them in classes. [A Voice—" Brooks."]

Books in the running brooks, sermons in stones,
And good in everything. [Laughter.]

I propose to indulge in no personalities ; they are not to my taste. I propose to deal in general principles.

Now, if my Irish friend be anywhere within the sound of my voice, he knows what is moving in this frame of mine, the son of an Irish father, who migrated in hot haste, and was chased into the port of New-York, his highest ambition being that his son might be born in America. [Great merriment.]

Some of my fellow-citizens of New-York, and some of my friends with whom
I quite agree about the absence of any necessity to violate the Constitution in
the matter of arrests, or otherwise, undertake to talk to me about freedom of
speech being suppressed. I would like to know when the time was in the history
of this country, for the last twenty years, that I could have dared to say in the
city of Charleston what a Southerner could say with impunity in this town?
[Loud applause.] My friends from Massachusetts must pardon me when I say
that for many years they have offended my Celtic prejudices by informing me
that we were all of the Anglo-Saxon race. I wish to be understood in regard to
that as the boys say about New-York, that "I don't see it," [laughter;] for
certainly none of those from whom I sprung have any connection with that
particular department of human distribution. [Laughter.] A distinguished
representative of the United States at the Court of St. James told them that
the people of this country felt more interest in the prosperity of London than of
New-York. I will not mention the name—but I will say that he did not belong
to this State. What offends me most is the expression of those Englishmen on
our Territory who dare, in their customary aping of the language and deport-
ment of their superiors, to cavil about the arms and progress of the country in
which they find a place so far superior to any they could be permitted to enjoy
in their own land. [Applause.] They are invited to clubs by gentlemen, and
they lie about them in saying they throw dice for drink, where dice never were
known. They are spies, and pimps, and eavesdroppers who are admitted to
circles of private society, and go out and write letters saying there was one thing
wanting. And so there was—a sturdy servant to kick the inquisitive vagabond
into the street. [Laughter and applause.] They hang around the purlieus of
our towns and drink their ale—which they very seldom pay for themselves—and
then turn up their snub-noses and open their ugly mouths to abuse a country
in which they are entertained. [Applause.] We are a patient people, but I
hope to God that the last illustration of that kind imported to this country will
prove that the goods are not credited to this market, and we do not mean to
have Englishmen insult us under any circumstances whatever. [Applause.]

I will differ with the majority here, in reference to one thing. Great apprehen-
sions are entertained lest England should interfere. I have prayed to God, on
my bended knees, that she would. [Loud applause.]

Let her but exhibit one single manifestation in that direction, and there is not
a man of my race that would talk about the exemption of forty-five years of age.
[Great laughter.] He would hobble on his crutch, in the ardent expectation of
splitting the head of any one who undertook to interfere in a matter that belongs to ourselves.

Permit me, however, to do justice to those wise, excellent and patriotic gentlemen of England who have been so just toward us, throughout this controversy.
I would disgrace myself, and insult you, if I did not acknowledge here my

gratitude to those who, without fear or hope of reward, have stood by our cause. I would do myself injustice if I did not admire the character of that great man, John Bright, [loud applause,] whose last observation in regard to *The London Herald* and *Standard* is, that he does not care much about their censure, for neither of them, in the markets of England, could affect the price of a pinch of snuff. [Laughter and applause.] The single reason, as you all know, why France and England desire, if they dared, to interfere in this fight, is the acknowledgment which they must make in the presence of the world, that they are indebted to us for the means of employing and supporting their population. [Applause.] One hundred thousand men in Lancashire maintained by public charity when I last spoke to an audience assembled!—One hundred thousand . men!—Which led me to make the proposition, to which I challenge any contradiction, that wild and fierce and blind as the rebels are, each division of this Union, in its armed presentation, is greater than the power of England! [Applause.] I was happy to discover that what fell from lips so obscure as mine, provoked a whole editorial column from a Manchester paper. They said that no American could have uttered a sentiment of that kind, and they recognized in the name of "Brady" one of those Irish Anglo-Phobian Papists who have been controlling the destinies of this country. [Laughter.] I think if that editor was here he would hardly suppose that I had religion enough to control anybody; or if I had, that it would control such an assemblage as this. [Laughter.]

Now, fellow-citizens, I am met everywhere, as you are, by the question, How is this thing to end? I am sorry to say that the satisfactory answer to that question is interfered with by two classes of human beings. First, by the women of this country. Bachelor as I am, no doubt this remark will subject me to censure. But I say, if the women of the North had manifested that interest which they should in the success of our cause—which the women of the South have done in theirs—thousands more of men would have been stimulated to take their position in the field. Then there is a class of my fellow-citizens who sneer at the misfortunes of our army, and manifest, to their utter disgrace, something like pleasure at the prosperity of our foes. I can never find myself *en rapport*, as the French say, with that class of people. [Cheers.] What is this war about? It certainly has grown into a war; it certainly is a war of the North against the South. And when I talked with Southerners, as I did with three in Philadelphia last Sunday, as ardent Secessionists and as bitter opponents as I can find anywhere—as bitter as those who cluster in presence of Jefferson Davis himself—I said, "Gentlemen, you must admit that there is a moral superiority in the people with whom I am associated, when you can talk to me freely what I would not dare to say at the South, except at the peril of my existence." [Applause.] And I said to them what I say to you: How is this thing to end? I say, with your permission, gentlemen, to my friends of the Democratic party, whom I cannot meet one by one on the street, and who perhaps would not value my opinion if I did—Sir, how do you propose to end it? The South say to you, "You are all Yankees; we propose no association with you, and will consent to none." Have you ever seen a man with a white face upon him or a black face upon him who would pursue for the sake of society the person who spurned him? [Cheers.] You ask me how this is to end. With the feeble powers that I have possessed since I arrived at man's estate, I have struggled for that which I would contend for if the Constitution were restored or continued, that is every right which the South can justly claim under that sacred instrument. But they say, we will make no peace. They propose that there shall be two governments on this soil—armed governments. Sir, I cannot consent to any such condition. ["No!"] Rome and Sparta, Carthage and Athens, were all republics; this was taught to you in your primer. Each of them was a military power. I refer you to *The Federalist* and the articles of Alexander Hamilton in regard to the possibility of maintaining separate organizations of government on this continent. When you can answer them, let me see your treatise or hear your discourse, and I will be submissive, as I hope I have always been, to the voice of reason. But, Mr. Southerner, listen to me and the men who have stood by the South, against the denunciations of presses—and, gentlemen, I see them represented on this platform—listen to me who, with the feeble capacity that I possess, have insisted always that you should have all the rights to which you are entitled. You say no—Mr. Lincoln was elected President. But you went into the canvass. He was chosen President, and yet there was a majority in both branches of Congress against him. I defy you to point out a single act of the Government which should have provoked any hostility on your part. But as long as there is breath in my body—if you make it a question between the South and the North—I should think I was unworthy of the mother who bore me if I did not go for any portion sustained by the Constitution of the United States. [Applause.]

And now, gentlemen, in conclusion, I propose to answer that question to my Southern friends: What will come of this war? You say you will never consent to be united with us. We say that we will never agree to the existence of two military Governments arising out of the same people on the same territory. The issue is distinct. [Cheers.] How is this to be resolved?

I will tell you, gentlemen, my opinion, and yet many here, in accordance with that difference of opinion to which I have referred, will differ with me. I have said, in the earlier part of my remarks, that there were some qualities of the New England character which did not commend themselves to my special regard. At the same time, you will permit me to say, that the most disinterested acts of friendship which I have ever received have been from people opposed to me in political sentiment. [Uproar near the door. "Go on!" "Go on!"] Oh, I will go on. That is no more than one single raid of a small lot of rebels. [Cheers and laughter.] My opinion is founded upon this. I remember on an occasion when we celebrated St. Patrick's Day—a circumstance to which I never had any special objection—when we made punch for others and Judys of ourselves, and still grew warm in the glow of social intercourse—Gen. Shields [cheers] made this remark, that wherever the Yankee located a blacksmith-shop, a tavern, or a school-house, he never was known to recede from it. [Cheers.] Can you remember any instance to the contrary? Why, half-way between Cairo and Suez, on the Grand Desert, a Yankee opened a house to introduce the travelers of that region to an institution called buckwheat-flour slapjacks, [laughter,] and had them cooked to a nicety by a regular and monotonous tick of a Yankee clock. [Laughter and cheers.] And if we ever come to the position called the falling-off place, we shall find a Yankee there, sitting on the brink, with his legs hanging over, and looking off and sighing, not, like Alexander, for new worlds to conquer, but that this world is so small. [Applause and laughter.]

Now I tell my Southern friends, from the place which I occupy, in regard to their property and their institution which they call slavery—which, unlike many in this assemblage, I would propose to retain to them under the Constitution of the United States—that their only chance is to let the Constitution be their guide, for if these Yankees once get down into that Southern territory, (who have a theory about this war,) and put arms into the hands of the negroes, [loud cheering,] and put up their long feet on the tables of the estates of which they take possession, I don't want to be the lawyer employed in an action of ejectment. [Great laughter and applause.] I sincerely believe that unless the gentlemen of the South will manifest some lingering remnant of attachment to the Union, and agree that the Constitution of the United States shall preserve us as one people in the territory that we occupy, the end of this war will be occupation : and Mr. Eli Thayer, whom I have never had the pleasure of seeing, in advance of me has illustrated the fact, that whenever you show any place to the Yankee to go to, he goes there, and when he goes there he stays there, and when they propose to remove him they find it exceedingly difficult. [Cheers.] You will pardon me for relating an anecdote. A man in a hotel in New Orleans heard his friend in the next room, who was subject to nightmare, making a fearful noise. He went in and said, "Why, you are in a dreadful state!" "Why, I am frightened," answered his friend : "I have had a dreadful dream!" "Did you dream of death?" "Worse than that." "Did you dream of the devil?" "Worse than that." "Well, then, what did you dream of?" "I thought I was back in the State of Maine?" [Great laughter.] That class of people can never be defeated. I am sorry to say it, I am an unwilling witness, and I hope my Teutonic friends, to whom the first speaker alluded, will excuse me when I say that neither whisky punch nor lager beer will ever overcome those iconoclasts. When civilization began in the East, it pursued its way over all the ruins of empire. Before I saw the ruins of the Old World I thought I should shed a tear over them, but when I discovered that they were the great stepping-stones by which humanity advances to the high position that it deserves to occupy, the ruin became to me a pleasure. Here civilization has found its last resting-place. There is no place to which to go back; civilization knows no regurgitation, it has no refluent wave. The people of the South in the single State of Virginia would never employ the necessary physical power to redeem that exhausted soil. Nobody will say, after my discourse closes, that I have been very eulogistic to the Yankee; but seriously, in the presence of my God, in the exercise of the best capacities that I know now to employ, I say to my friends of the South, however gallant and chivalric, and persevering may be their struggle in the field, all history will be false, all analogies fallacious, every promise to the human race an absurdity, if this people, who have conquered the barren East and conquered the ocean, and are willing to encounter all circumstances of privation, shall not own the whole of this continent before this country expires. [Loud and continued applause.]

---

## SPEECH OF DAVID DUDLEY FIELD, ESQ.

DAVID DUDLEY FIELD was then introduced by the Mayor, amid applause. He said:—

MR. CHAIRMAN AND FELLOW-CITIZENS,—It was my expectation, as it was my wish, that this meeting should be addressed chiefly by speakers whose political affinities were with parties other than that which placed this administration in power; and such, I understand, Mr. Chairman, is the arrangement. It was thought best, however, not to leave it wholly so, but that all parties should be represented in the proceedings. There is a common ground on which we all can stand, [cheers;] and that is a firm, unfaltering purpose, to put down this rebellion by force of arms;—[applause]—by force of arms, and I will add, by force of arms alone. [Cheers.] Other questions may be postponed and laid aside. Who got us into this war, how we got into it, and who is responsible for it;—these are questions about which my friends who have spoken, and who are to speak, and myself, may differ; but these are questions that we can settle hereafter. Now we have something else to do. [Cheers.] Then, there are questions about the manner in which this war has been heretofore conducted. They think that it should have been conducted in one way, I in another, and you, perhaps, in still another; but that question can also be settled hereafter.

The past is past, irrevocably past. We will leave it now, and recur to it hereafter. To-day we stand together, agreed upon this proposition, that there is but one way to peace, and that way is through earnest, grim, victorious war.

## SPEECH OF HON. JUDGE DALY.

MAYOR OPDYKE.—A little while ago you had the pleasure of being addressed by an Irishman whom the Rebels have changed into a Yankee; you will now be addressed by an Irishman who was born a Yankee—Judge DALY. [Cheering.]

Judge DALY said :—Listening, like yourselves, fellow-citizens, to the resolutions that have just been read, I find they answer the question which I rose to ask : What is the duty of Northern men, without distinction of party, in this crisis of the country ? [Applause.] That is the absorbing question, not only with the mass of upturned faces I see before me, but with that greater audience spread over the land, awaiting the issue of the contest now going on.

I propose in a very few words—for the hour is late, and it is my duty to be brief—to address myself to that question, and to do it with all the sincerity which grows out of my own deep convictions, and with a wide toleration for the difference of opinion that may be entertained upon a question so momentous. [Applause.] There are a number of men in the North at present, who talk of peace, of an armistice, of concession, who hope for compromise, and who have no hope of the war. If persons of that temper have made up their minds that the war is hopeless, and that the separation of the States in revolt is inevitable, then their conduct and declarations are consistent with their convictions ; but to the men who advocate the adoption of such measures now as the only means for the restoration of the Union, for the preservation of the land in the territorial unity in which it was left to us by our fathers—I say to such men, that if they entertain the conviction that a resort to such measures now will restore the Union, I have little faith in their foresight, or if they possess it, I do not believe in their sincerity. [Cheers.] As long, in my judgment, as the States now in rebellion think it possible to separate, they will think of nothing else. They will continue to think it possible while they can keep an army in the field ; and as long as they know or feel that they have any military strength, every suggestion tending toward the re-establishment of the Union by a proffer of peace, of concession, or of an armistice, unless some distinct proposal comes in the first instance from them, is the wildest of northern delusions. Our course is a plain one, to break down their military strength. This we can or we cannot do. If we cannot, then we must submit to what is inevitable. If we can, and in my judgment we will, if not interfered with by foreign nations, we shall have accomplished our task, for matters afterward will adjust themselves more easily under our form of government than under any other.

This struggle, fellow-citizens, is for the preservation of our institutions, for the maintenance of republican government, and to all truly patriotic men that feature gives to the contest its deep earnestness and intensity. We have but to take up the morning paper of to-day and read the difference of exchange and the premium upon gold. What does that indicate? That unerring barometer shows the judgment entertained in the moneyed circles of the world of the possibility of preserving the American Republic. [Cheers.] And the doubt, uncertainty, and hesitation, which the people who live in other lands entertain of the possibility of our being able to do so, tends to lessen the value of the circulating medium of the country, because accompanied by the conviction, that if the Southern States separate, the Union is at an end; that the Northern States will separate also among themselves, acting upon the instinct of their individual interest, and being restrained no longer by the tie of the Union. This, I say, is the growing conviction abroad, and it is increased in magnitude by every Northern voice of dissent. If we have any hope at all for the preservation of this country, that hope lies in the continuous, the unabating, and the vigorous prosecution of the war. [Loud cheers.]

I am not now giving voice to the excitement which a public speaker may be supposed to feel in the presence of a large body of his fellow-citizens. I am giving outward, distinct and direct utterance to the conviction that has been in my mind since the war began, since the first shot was fired upon Sumter, since the American flag was first insulted; and everything in the course of events has tended to convince me that there is no hope for the preservation of this nation, except in the vigorous prosecution of this war. [Cheers.] We may differ as to the means by which it may be most effectually prosecuted, and I, no doubt, differ with a large number who are here. This is no place to discuss that difference, and I do not intend to do so. I am here to speak for myself, and I speak for no other man. I do not propose to imitate the egregious egotism of a gentleman, who said publicly the other day that he spoke for one-fourth of the United States— the whole people of the West—and that they were opposed to the prosecution of the war.

There may be great evils in this war. War is always an evil. But allow me to say that there have been greater evils afflicting a nation than civil war. Civil war, while it destroys weak nations, strengthens strong ones. [Cheers] The stalwart, permanent and vigorous English Constitution grew out of two hundred years of civil war. Civil war has made France what it is. Civil war has almost restored the past grandeur of Spain. If it has destroyed weak republics like those of South America, it is because they come within the general terms of the proposition I have stated. [Applause.]

The conviction on the mind of every discerning Northern man must be that which has been expressed by one of the speakers, that the result of this war is simply a question of time. We cannot now conjecture or fathom what will be the duration of it; but, so far as one may speak of the future, advised by the experience of the past, the result of it is certain, except in the event of foreign intervention. How, let me ask, is foreign intervention to be prevented?

4

There are many persons who apprehend the interference of the French nation, and there are indications enough to satisfy us, that, did they deem it possible or prudent to interfere, and open our blockade, that the Governments of France and England would do so. Let me say to those who are not in favor of the further prosecution of this war, and who talk of an armistice, that they can give no greater encouragement to those who desire to interfere in our affairs, than by proclaiming and advocating such measures. [Cheers.] The strongest bulwark we can raise for the preservation of the nation is the union of the Northern people in one sentiment—that, whatever may be their differences of opinion, growing out of the past history of the country, or as to the mode in which the war has hitherto been conducted, there is no difference as to the duty of prosecuting this war to its ultimate result. [Loud applause.]

I have only one word more to say, because I am unwilling to trespass on the patience of so large an audience—[cries of "Go on"]—and that is, that war is a stern teacher. Individuals and nations learn from it what they would never learn without it; and we of the North and of the South—of this at present divided, but hereafter, I hope, to be united and compact nationality—will learn a lesson from it which we would not have learned otherwise. Mr. Brady has alluded to Cato, in the course of his remarks. It brought to my mind the reply of Cato to Cæsar, as we find it in Sallust, describing the state of the Roman people, at the time of the gigantic conspiracy of Cataline. Cato described the condition of the Roman people—very much like the state we were in when this war began. He said that they were a people so given to the acquisition of wealth, as to be indifferent to everything else; that virtue, integrity, and zeal in the public service were followed by no reward; that there was, in consequence, great poverty in the State, and great wealth in the individual members composing it; that virtue, capacity or experience were not the qualities for which men were elevated to important public trust, but that everything was open to political ambition; and he added, that it was no wonder that Cataline—that ancient secessionist, who undertook to do what the people of the Southern States are now attempting—to overthrow the government of his fathers—had succeeded so far, for, when the people thought of nothing but their individual interest, when every one was struggling to get money, and indulging in the luxuries incident to its possession, it was not surprising, when an attack was made upon the State, that it should be found weak, and unable to defend itself. [Applause.] We have all, in my judgment, learned this lesson from the war. Many, like myself, have not been satisfied with a great deal that has been done by this Government, and in the exercise of our individual judgment would have had it otherwise. We have complained of the want of capacity and of the absence of the most ordinary experience; but if those whom we elect are not as capable as they ought to be, whom have we to fix the blame upon? We have to fix it upon a system of political machinery, by which experience, capacity and virtue are regarded as nothing, in comparison to the qualities which will serve the ends of the political organism. Everything is subordinate to the means which that machinery employs to thrust into places of high public trust those of whom the least is known. [Loud cheers.] We have something to learn from that ; and if we get out of this war, delivered from this political Juggernaut which strangles individual opinion—which crushes out all independence of thought and of action—which gives no man the right to exercise individual views except as a part of this machinery—if we do nothing more in the war than to overthrow this system, we shall liberate ourselves from—what has become in its general operation—a practical, and at the same time an irresponsible, despotism. [Cheers.] I speak not especially of any political party, because, as you all know, it belongs to the Republican and the Democratic party alike. [Applause.]

The question may be asked, why have I for a long time acted as a public man, discharging a public trust, to which I have been indebted to the machinery of party? I can answer by saying, that in the many years that I have held this trust I was never in a public meeting, Democratic or Republican, or in one that had anything of a political character. A friend behind me suggests that this is not a political meeting. I did not mean to be understood in that sense ; for I have had the honor of addressing my fellow-citizens at the grand Union Mass Meeting in April. I meant a party meeting. I have abstained, because I did not think it right for a Judge to mingle in the active organization of party politics. But if I had been free to act then, it would have made no difference ; for so thoroughly had both parties become organized by this system of machinery ; so completely had it taken root, that a man enclosed in a pyramid might as well expect to be heard, when he cried aloud, as for any public man in this country to raise his voice in protest against a system common to both political parties, and which was rapidly bringing the nation to destruction. This, if I understand it, is no party meeting. It is a national one, called in view of the impending peril of the whole country. Allow me to say, it would be far from me to intimate that there was anything in the expressions which have fallen from the speakers, or in the responses that have been made by those who listened to them, of a party character ; and I would to God, that in this contest there had been more examples of such toleration, forbearance and love of unity. [Prolonged cheers.]

I can only, in conclusion, condense all I would say in a single historical allusion. When Admiral Blake was fighting the battles of his country on the ocean, under the government of a man whom he did not respect, he returned an answer to his men which, in my judgment, ought to be the answer given by every loyal American, with regard to his course in this contest : "It is our duty," he said, "to stand by the Government under which we live, and fight for its supremacy, maintenance and preservation, no matter in whose hands, temporarily, the Government may be." [Enthusiastic cheers.]

Loud calls were then made for "Van Buren," and upon being introduced Hon. John Van Buren spoke as follows:—

### SPEECH OF MR. VAN BUREN.

Mr. Chairman and Fellow-Citizens,—I beg to return you my sincere thanks for the kindness with which you have received me to-night. I received some days since an invitation from several respectable gentlemen, with some of whom I have been for some time acquainted, to attend this meeting to-night, and to address those who should be here assembled. I was notified that General Winfield Scott would preside, and I regret to learn that the state of his health, as was somewhat anticipated by the Committee who invited me—that the state of his health has proved to be such that he has been unable to attend. His place, however, is well supplied by the Mayor of your city, who is the presiding officer on this occasion. [Applause.] I was also informed of the resolutions that it was proposed to pass, and a copy of them was inclosed in the invitation I received to address you. I was requested to look at these resolutions, and unless I expressed some dissent, I was notified I would be considered as assenting to them and to the use of my name. In looking over the resolutions it seemed to me that, with some verbal and unimportant corrections, they are perfectly proper to be adopted, and I so stated to the gentlemen who invited me. I saw nothing in the resolutions, in the character of the gentlemen who invited me to attend, in the character or public career of the presiding officer, that prevented my cordial participation in the proceedings of the meeting, and I therefore unconditionally accepted. [Applause.] If there is anything, as has often been suggested, beyond this as the object of this meeting, it is unknown to me ; and I think it proper thus to state at the outset the extent to which I have been connected with the originating of the meeting, and the extent of the responsibility I propose to assume in coming here with you to-night. I came in while Mr. Brady was speaking, and derived the greatest pleasure and satisfaction from his remarks, and there was nothing in the remarks of the gentleman who followed him that would cause me any uneasiness. I have, therefore, every reason to believe that our proceedings here to-night thus far are acceptable, and I hope they will be such as will promote the cause of the country which we all claim to have at heart. Now you will allow me to state with a little particularity what has been my position in reference to the questions that have been agitated before the people during the last three or four months, and although I have an alarming amount of papers here—[laughter]—what I have to say will consume but a reasonable amount of your time. In the outset I desire to call your attention to the position I assumed here on the 13th of October last, when we were about to enter upon a political campaign such as the constitution and laws authorize previous to the regular election in November of each year. Two candidates had been nominated for Governor. One was Mr. Wadsworth, and the other Mr. Seymour. The friends of Mr. Seymour assembled here to ratify his nomination, and to take such measures as they deemed expedient to promote his election. I was invited to be present and address them. For three years previously I had never anywhere addressed my fellow-citizens, as during a part of that time my health was such as to preclude the possibility of my doing so. On that occasion I took the liberty of stating what were the views that I entertained in reference to the condition of the country. I said that in entering into this controversy there were a great many who, I had no doubt, would agree with me in being governed solely by one consideration in following out whatever could be done for a vigorous prosecution of this war. As to the thing that should be done at this election, if I believed—and I said so with entire truth and sincerity—if I believed that by voting for Wadsworth I should contribute to the success of our arms, and bring about an honorable peace, I should vote for Mr. Wadsworth for Governor without hesitation ; but it was because I did not so believe, because I was entirely confident that such a course would not be advantageous to the country, and would not bring about an honorable peace—which is the legitimate object of war—that I should support Mr. Seymour. I also said on that occasion, in speaking of the advantages of supporting Mr. Seymour, that my object was to sustain the President as far as justice will authorize, and sustain him in every fair governmental measure that he may adopt for the purpose of carrying on the war or to uphold the government. I said that it was our purpose to stand by the Union and the constitution, and to stand by Mr. Lincoln as far as he would let us, and to stand by McClellan whether he would let us or not. [Mingled applause, hisses, and great confusion.] Now, in conclusion—[renewed hisses and applause]—I am only repeating what I said to you on the 13th of October. [Cries of "Go on."] I said, "Protract this contest to the next Presidential election, no matter what is the result, this country will be irretrievably swamped long before we reach the 4th of March, 1865. It must be done sooner—the result must be achieved under Lincoln ; it must be achieved by giving vigor to him in resisting what I am sure he feels disposed to resist—the demands of the abolitionists. Stand by him. He is a cross of Kentucky on Illinois, and cannot be an abolitionist. [Applause.] Let the great State of New-York, on the 4th of November, (as I have every reason to hope the States of Pennsylvania, Ohio and Indiana will to-morrow,) show what her principles are. And let you and I meet here, after the election, and unite in shouting that New-York is redeemed." It will be observed that then I stated that party organization had ceased to be of any practical importance ; that the sole inquiry, in my judgment, was how should we best carry on the war—(A Voice, "That's so"]—and that I would be governed entirely in that canvass by that single consideration. [Applause.] What I then said I repeated in various portions of the State after the 13th of October, and until the very day of the election. Governor Seymour was present on this stand at the time I spoke. He was with me in Brooklyn, in Rochester and in Buffalo, and the single complaint his friends made, as far as I understood, was that I fell far short in my support of the war, of the vigorous and determined support that Mr. Seymour expressed his resolution to give to it under all circumstances. [Applause.] The election came and passed, and it is no part of our province or purpose to consider the particular result, except to say that the people of the State of New-York, after a very active canvass, were about equally divided—for to speak of a majority of a few thousand in a poll of six hundred and odd thousand is simply to say that they were about equally divided. And the same was true of the States of Ohio, Indiana and Pennsylvania; the majority in these great Central States was trifling, and to-day, to-night, while we are here, the people of these great central and controlling portions of these United States may very properly be regarded as about evenly divided between the two parties that were organized at the last canvass, and future results will depend, in my humble judgment, a great deal more upon the future conduct of individuals than upon anything that has transpired in the past. [Applause.] Now we have passed through the election. There is no election in this State till next Autumn. We are assembled on the 6th of March to determine, not what New Hampshire shall do, not what Connecticut shall do, but what the people of the city of New-York and of this State shall do. And there being no election pending, I hold it to be entirely preposterous to assume that people who differed during the last canvass in this State, may not unite cordially in such measures as may be necessary to put down a rebellion that has no shadow of justification. [Applause.] Under such circumstances I have been called upon by a Committee of highly respectable gentlemen to redeem the pledges made in the campaign, in the very place where I now stand, and if I was in truth, as I then declared I was, in favor of a vigorous prosecution of the war, and if I did truly believe that the interest of the country far transcended in importance any political or party organization that was in existence, now to come forward and say so in common with those who belonged to a different political party. [Applause.] Such being the fact, I have no hesitation in saying that I cordially agree to the resolutions that have been adopted. [Applause.] I am for the vigorous prosecution of the war. [Applause.] I am for the prosecution of the war until this rebellion is wholly overthrown. [Applause.] I am for destroying the usurped government that has been set up over the Southern States, and this thing that calls itself a Confederate Government, and until that is done, I hold that all propositions for peace are entirely preposterous and absurd. [Applause.] Now being for the war, I am necessarily with everybody that is for the war; and being opposed to peace, I am necessarily opposed to everybody that is for peace. [Applause.] [A Voice.—" How about the wayward sisters?" Great laughter.]

Mr. Van Buren.—Now, how did the war begin? Without stopping to discuss disputed propositions—that would be of no avail—there is no doubt that there has been, for a great length of time, a large number of politicians in the South who have been determined to extend Slavery to the free territory of the United States. They endeavored to use the organization of the Democratic party for that purpose, and, in 1848, they assumed such a position in regard to it, as to force what I considered the regular Democracy of the State of New-York out of the Democratic party. [Applause.] The elections of '48, and '52, and '56 came and passed. The election of 1860 was the next that transpired, and, in the mean time, this disposition was manifested by various efforts to force Slavery into Kansas, and other measures that it is not necessary now to discuss, and to which I was always opposed. In 1860, in the Democratic Convention, they declared that the platform of the Convention should contain a recognition of the legality of Slavery in all the territories of the United States ; and they declared, in addition, that Slavery should be protected by the General Government in all the territories belonging to the Union. The Democracy of the North refused to agree to that, and the Convention broke up. It reassembled at Baltimore, and again broke up, and the election of 1860 came on, the Southern men having a candidate of their own, and the Northern and Western Democracy generally supporting Mr. Douglas, and a large number of gentlemen supporting Mr. Lincoln, resulting in the election of Mr. Lincoln. [Applause.] In that contest I took no part. I voted, but I did nothing more. No man ever heard me, in public or in private, express any opinion in regard to it, except when the election came off, I deposited my vote in opposition to Mr. Lincoln. [Voices.—"Good."] After that election, Congress assembled. Mr. Lincoln's message declared in the fullest manner his unwillingness to interfere with Slavery in the States. It recognized, to the fullest extent, the right of the different States to have Slavery if they chose, and his entire indisposition to interfere with it. Notwithstanding that, several States seceded from the Union, as they said. They held a convention, and resolved themselves out. Their representatives abandoned their seats in Congress, although they had control of the Senate and House of Representatives, and the Supreme Court of the United States. They retired from the Congress of the United States. They went further and set up a government of their own, or said they did. Now you all remember the debates between Webster and Hayne upon the subject of the right to secede from the Union. Mr. Webster told Mr. Hayne what has since proven true—that that was mere rebellion, and when they put it in operation, they would see that, in order to carry out what they assumed to be the right of peaceful secession and nullification, they must use force, and be met by force, and the law of the strongest must decide the controversy. [Applause.] This occurred. They assumed to set up a government. They formed a Congress and elected a President. But they were not content with this. They seized the property of the United States—they seized its forts, its ships, its treasure. They fired upon the flag of the United States at Fort Sumter, and claimed the right to exercise the power of a sovereign government. Now, you will bear in mind—every fair-minded man in the United States will bear in mind—that up to this moment not one hair of their heads had been injured. No right of any Southern man had been invaded. History will record that the world never witnessed a rebellion against a governmental authority before, where the rebels could not lay their finger upon a thing to show that either their property, their liberty, or their rights had been, in the slightest particular, invaded. [Great applause.] This being the fact, the city of New-York sent forth eighty thousand men to quell this rebellion. Her capitalists advanced three hundred millions of dollars to put down this rebellion. The State of New-York sent two hundred thousand men. Now am I to argue, in view of these facts and the past history of this contest, that the rebellion is atrociously unjust, and that the war in which we have engaged with the South is rightfully prosecuted by us in vindication of the Constitution and the Union. [Applause.] Now, what is the condition of this contest? They were not satisfied with what I have detailed, but they announced they were going to establish a Republic, the corner-stone of which should be Slavery, and they are now engaged in that task—in endeavoring to establish a Republic on this continent, in 1863, the corner-stone of which shall be Slavery. Now, I went to Herkimer in 1847, to lay a corner-stone, but it was not this. [Laughter.] It was as much unlike this as anything you can possibly imagine, and it adds no additional attractions to the contest, as far as I am concerned, that they should avow this object in prosecuting the war. It is now a contest forced upon the non-slaveholding and loyal slaveholding States, by those who are endeavoring to build up a Republic based on Slavery. *To prostrate a rebellion that has that object in view, I am willing to devote any means, any time, any exertions within my power, during the rest of my life.* [Applause, and three cheers.] Now let us see whether there is anything worth considering in what is suggested by those who dissent from us, and are unwilling to prosecute this war. The measures that have been recently adopted by Congress are so lately adopted, that it becomes any man who is careful what he says, to be guarded in speaking of them. The President issued two proclamations—both of them, as I have frequently stated, I disapproved. He issued both before I spoke on the 13th of October, and before Governor Seymour spoke. Neither of us saw anything in them which prevented us from favoring a vigorous prosecution of the war. If there was nothing then, it is certain that there is nothing now. [Applause.] One of the bills which has excited the sensibility of several gentlemen who have spoken in New Jersey, and at a certain ball in this city, [hisses,] is a bill which gives extraordinary powers over the purse and the sword to the President of the United States. Another is a bill which seeks to protect by indemnity the President and those connected with him from claims for damages for arrests they have made. They are opposed to another bill, as I understand, which has become the law, which authorizes the President, in his discretion, to suspend the writ of *habeas corpus.* [Applause.] I will state now, as briefly as I can, what are my views in regard to this. In the first place, as to the bill which gives the President power over the sword and the purse, I agree that it makes him almost a dictator. I agree that it is a very great stretch of power. A VOICE.—" He ought to have it."

I agree that, unless there may be a necessity for it, it should not be done. Everybody knows that in prosecuting a war under a republican government, which consists of several States, the great apprehension is that there may not be unity on the part of the States sufficient to impart energy to the national Executive head. That was predicted as one of the grounds upon which our system of government would fail. I call the attention of my democratic friends to this, because there seems to be particular solicitude on this point now. [Laughter.] The President was given the power of the purse and the sword in 1839, when Great Britain had directed forcible possession to be taken of a portion of the State of Maine, and Sir John Harvey had moved troops of Great Britain into that territory to hold it. The Governor of the State of Maine met this action by moving Maine troops on to the same territory. The President of the United States called the attention of Congress to it, and left it to their wisdom to say what ought to be done. Now I hold in my hand a copy of the bill that they passed upon that occasion, in 1839. I will state to you the substance of the various sections, without detaining you at this late hour by reading the bill. The first section puts the whole naval and military force of the United States, and the militia, at the disposal of the President. [Applause.] The second declares that the militia, when called out, shall be compelled to serve six months. The third gives the President power to call out fifty thousand volunteers. In those days, when our army had never reached eight thousand men, it was a weighty matter to call out fifty thousand men, and was regarded as an enormous authority. [Laughter.] The fourth section gives the President power to complete and employ all the armed vessels of the United States—putting the whole army and navy of the United States at his disposal. [Applause.] The fifth section appropriates ten millions of dollars to carry into effect the provisions of this act. In those days ten millions of dollars was a great deal of money. [Laughter.] The sixth section appropriates eighteen thousand dollars to send a special minister to Great Britain. The seventh section authorizes him to expend a million of dollars in finishing the fortifications upon our sea-board and arming them. The eighth section directs that the militia and volunteers, when called out, shall be portions of the Army of the United States. Now, how do you suppose that bill passed? It put the whole purse and sword into the absolute power of the President of the United States. Clay, Webster and Calhoun—men of ability, though, perhaps, inferior to the Solons of our day, [laughter,] were members of the Senate. The bill passed the Senate, and these three statesmen—

although all violently opposed personally and politically to the then President of the United States—voted for the bill, and if passed the Senate unanimously. [Applause.] It passed the House of Representatives, after a full discussion, by a vote of 201 to 6, and the leader of that six was Henry A. Wise, [hisses,] the bold brigadier who distinguished himself so greatly at Nag's Head, [laughter.] while his brigade was fighting on Roanoke Island. [Applause.] Now let us see whether the democracy of that day was alarmed at this union of the purse and the sword, and, in the first place, let us see how the political opponents of the administration treated it. Governor Seward was then Governor of the State of New-York, having been elected in 1838, and a political opponent of the President. On the 7th of March he communicated this act to the Legislature, with a most praiseworthy message, concluding thus :—"I respectfully call your attention to this subject, with the expectation that an expression on our part of concurrence in the policy of the general government will contribute to avert the calamities of war, and cause a speedy and honorable adjustment of the difficulties between this country and Great Britain." Mr. Isaac L. Varian was then Chairman of the Democratic General Committee, and Mr. Elijah F. Purdy was one of the Secretaries. They called a meeting of the democrats of this city, and over that meeting Mr. Holmes presided, and for Vice-Presidents were men whose names, when read to any democrat, will bring back associations of great interest, and perhaps of some sadness, unless he supposes that the prominent democrats in the city now are more respectable than those whose names I will read. The Vice-Presidents were Henry Yates, Walter Bowne, Samuel Tappan, Myndert Van Schaick, Gideon Tucker, Abraham Van Nest, Gilbert Coutant; and they resolved, not that there was danger in the union of the purse and the sword—not that it was a usurpation—but that it was a " prompt and patriotic measure" on the part of the House of Representatives. [Loud cheers.] Let us see how it was received by the electors. It was on the 2d and 3d days of March, as I have stated to you. The election in New Hampshire came on then, as it will now, within a few days after the adjournment of Congress ; and New Hampshire, which had been somewhat equally divided, gave seven thousand majority for the democratic ticket. I shall be pleased if my democratic friends find it gives as large a majority now. [Cheers and laughter.] The city of New-York, by a defection of the conservative portion of the democracy, had been thrown into the hands of what was then called the Whigs. The city election almost immediately followed, and the city was recovered. Isaac L. Varian was elected Mayor by a thousand majority, and twelve out of seventeen wards gave democratic majorities, immediately after this extraordinary usurpation. General Scott, who was to have presided here this evening, fortunately for the country, was then prominent in the command of the armies of the United States. On the 7th of March he went to Maine, and he remained there until about the 21st, when he concluded an arrangement with Lieutenant-Governor Harvey, by which the British troops retired from their position in the State of Maine, the Maine troops also retired, and civil officers were left in protection of the public property, and, by his wisdom and his foresight, by the 24th of March he was able to report to the government of the United States that the whole difficulty had passed over. [Applause.] Congress assembled in December, and the President of the United States made this communication to them:—

" The extraordinary powers vested in me by an act of Congress for the defence of the country in an emergency, considered so far probable as to require that the Executive should possess ample means to meet it, have not been exerted. They have therefore, been attended with no other result than to increase, by the confidence thus reposed in me, my obligations to maintain, with religious exactness, the cardinal principles that govern our intercourse with other nations. Happily, in our pending questions with Great Britain, out of which this unusual grant of authority arose, nothing has occurred to require its exertion; and as it is about to return to the Legislature, I trust that no future necessity may call for its exercise by them, or its delegation to another department of the government."

Not a dollar was expended, not a volunteer was called out, not a man from the militia was brought into the field under this act ; and I would be glad to know why it may not happen that this extraordinary demonstration on the part of the Congress of the United States, of the power and resources of the loyal portion of this Confederacy, may not again be followed by a similar auspicious result. The merciful way to prosecute a war is to make an overwhelming demonstration of strength, to satisfy those who are prepared to resist the rightful authority of the Government, that resistance is useless, and that they must be crushed [Cheers.] Now, gentlemen, there is nothing, in my humble judgment, therefore, in the law passed putting this enormous power in the possession of the President of the United States to deter me from assisting in a vigorous prosecution of the war. [Cheers.] I can very well understand how, if I sympathized with the rebellion—if I deemed that this war should fail—I could spend hours and columns in picking flaws in this act. But if I believed that substantial justice required—that the great ends of prosecuting the war demand that the whole power of the Government shall be lodged by the Congress of the United States in the President of the United States, I will bow in silence to the act, whether I approve of it or not. [Prolonged cheers.] If the President of the United States had usurped these powers, there might be a degree of propriety in denouncing it; but when the representatives of the people, legally elected, after due deliberation, assume the responsibility of lodging these trusts in him, in my humble judgment, and certainly in view of the precedent to which I have referred, no wise man will ever complain of the act. [Applause.] Now, in regard to the bill to indemnify the President of the United States for any damages in consequence of arrests that have been made. I have simply to say that if this act is constitutional it will protect him; if it is not, it will not. The courts are open to those complaining of arrests at any time, by prosecuting for damages they may have received. Again, as to the authorizing the President to suspend the *habeas corpus,* all of you who have paid any attention to my remarks heretofore, know my views in regard to the power of the President. I suppose he cannot suspend the *habeas corpus* under the Constitution of the United States. Chief-Justice Taney, in an opinion which I have never seen answered, has demonstrated it, and a republican judge in Wisconsin, Chief-Justice Dixon, who is now a republican candidate for re-election against the democratic candidate, has, in a recent decision, solemnly so adjudged, and, notwithstanding this, he is the republican candidate in Wisconsin for re-election. The Congress of the United States tacitly admit this by assuming that they must authorize the President to suspend the writ, and they have gone on to do so. I believe Congress is the party that should suspend the writ; they so judge, and they have authorized the President to suspend the writ, when he judged it wise and prudent to do so. I don't object to that law. [Loud cheers.] What I have to say in regard to that is, that I do not think it would be wise—I doubt very much whether the President and Congress have power—to suspend the writ in the State of New-York, and think you will see in a few moments, when I have very briefly stated my reasons for this view, that there is no need of any suspension of the writ of *habeas corpus* in this State.

The writ of *habeas corpus* is a writ by which a party imprisoned brings himself, or is brought, before a judge, to inquire into the causes of his detention, and if these causes are legal, if he is properly imprisoned, the judge remands him to prison. This is a right to which the people of this country, and the people of Great Britain, have always shown their devotion. It is unwise ever to unnecessarily suspend it. It is well to lodge this power in the President, to be exercised where hostilities are actually pending—to be exercised in parts in proximity to those where hostilities exist ; but here, where our courts are open, where our citizens are loyal, where it is entirely competent to bring up anybody who has committed any crime, and put him in prison, and, when he sues out his writ, to show that he ought to be detained, and then to remand him to prison, it would be unwise, in my judgment, to run counter to the prejudices of our people as to the Constitution, by suspending the writ. It has not been done yet. But those who do so will find that they have excited what a distinguished general calls a fire in the rear, which may be more troublesome than any fire they might have in front. It is not necessary. I know the people of the State of New-York. I know there is no occasion for any extraordinary remedies for enforcing the law. They are a loyal people ; trust them, and, my word for it, the result will show it. Now, gentlemen, this is all I have to say in regard to the measures of the last Congress, except simply to state, that there is nothing in the acts of Congress which calls upon me to hesitate for a single moment as to a vigorous prosecution of the war. I intended, however, to call your attention to the fact that the writ of *habeas corpus* was not suspended during the war of the Revolution, in the war of 1812, or in the war with Mexico, although there were great differences of opinion, and very strong statements made in opposition to the carrying on of the war. Yet the country prospered, and the war was successful. Now, then, allow me to say one thing more, because our object in coming here to-night is to consult freely, and that is the wisest way. And what I have to say is in reference to the proclamation of the President of the United States, declaring slaves free in certain parts of the Union. [Prolonged cheers.] I have taken occasion, on several times, to state (and that was perfectly known when I was invited to speak this evening) what my objections were to that proclamation. There are no objections to its constitutionality. The President has a right to make any proclamation he chooses. [applause,] and so have I. [Applause and laughter.] The only question I make is as to the wisdom and legal effect of this proclamation. Now, I say the proclamation does not set anybody free. If a man is free by law, he is free with or without the proclamation. But I say that it excites the Southern people to this view of the subject. [Hisses and applause mingled.] They say, " You declare that if we come back and submit to the law and to the Government, then our slaves are emancipated." That was not the President's intention. You may rely upon it. He did not emancipate the slaves in any territory of the United States that is under the dominion of the United States. They are not emancipated in Kentucky, in Missouri, in Tennessee, or in Maryland. [A Voice.—" They ought to be," followed by hisses, applause, and cries of " Order."] And that was, in my humble judgment, no part of his purpose. In my judgment, his sole object was to declare, as a general policy, that as our armies advanced against the rebels, when the rebels were conquered, their slaves should be legally free. There is no doubt about that, with or without the proclamation. Slavery exists by force, recognized by law ; slaves now are held in the so-called Confederate States by virtue of the Confederate States Governments and the Confederate United States authority. When our armies advance, and those governments are overthrown, the slaveholders who refuse to recognize the Constitution of the United States, lose their slaves by law beyond all peradventure. [Loud applause.] That being so, it is not wise, in my humble judgment, to issue such a declaration ; but that, of course, is a matter for the President. I say, as I have frequently said, that in my judgment, all the good that could have been done by it has been done. Now, then, gentlemen, another consequence is, that these Southern men ought to be led to see that their only hope for continuing slavery is by being in the Union. [A Voice.—" God forbid," followed by cheers and hisses.] That is their only protection, and it is for them to determine, under the Constitution, whether they will continue to avail themselves of it. Nor, gentlemen, if I were President, would I undertake to interfere with free discussion in the United States. Now there is no doubt that what is and what is not a fair limit for free discussion may be the subject of dispute. But the Constitution in the first article of the Amendments, prohibits Congress from passing any law to abridge freedom of speech. When a State Constitution authorizes an election, it authorizes discussion. I believe I have given the fullest evidence of that by discussing all over the State of New-York the action of the President and these different measures. Here, in the State of New-York, there is no occasion for it. I would not undertake to interfere with free discussion at a time when an election is pending. When there is no election pending, a different rule may prevail. [A Voice.—"Would you send the *World* to the army?"] I would do just as the army chose in reference to that. If the army like the *World*, I would let them take it; if they want the *Tribune*, I would let them take that. But let me tell you that it is entirely idle to undertake to fly in the face of the prejudices of the people. You have your own prejudices, I have mine, and others have theirs. No man can look over this State and the State of Ohio, Indiana, Illinois and Pennsylvania, and not see that, from some cause or other, there has been a great reaction in opposition to the policy of the war and the support of the President. That is clear by the canvass. No man can listen to the returns of the elections that come here every day from Troy, Utica, Rochester, Lockport, Oswego, Ithaca and Auburn, without seeing that, from some cause or other, the reaction that began last Fall has not ceased. Now, you who are prudent and wise men—who are in a position to advise the President of the United States, which I am not, and don't intend to be—[laughter]—must give him your opinion as to what he had better do. I have given such suggestions as I think will throw light upon the matter. Gentlemen, I believe that it is just as much our duty to unite in a vigorous prosecution of the war under the President of the United States as it was when the war was first declared, notwithstanding anything that may have been done. Nor am I one of those who insist that he should put a particular general in command of the army or any portion of it. I never suggested that he should make a change in his Cabinet, that one member should be put out and some other person take his place. That belongs to him, and I am not disposed to interfere. It is for him to determine how his responsibilities shall be discharged, and not me. But what I do say is, that he had better trust the people. I am one of those who am not in the habit of speaking of the people as something separate from myself. I very often meet men who tell me that the people want this or that. Well, I say, I guess not. I am one of the people, and I don't want it—and how do you get at the result? The only way I know of to determine what the people want, is to make up your mind what you want yourself, and then infer, in the absence of evidence to the contrary, that other people want the same thing. [Prolonged laughter.]

Now, there is great anxiety felt as to the course of the democrats. Gentlemen, a democrat is a peculiar institution. It does no good to drive the democrats—to bully or to attempt to intimidate them. They will have their own way. That was always their habit, as I have found. But I never shall be made to believe that the men who stood by George Clinton, or their fathers before them in the Revolution, who stood by Tompkins and Jackson in 1812, who stood by

Polk and Marcy in the Mexican war, will be found wanting in this. It remains to be seen whether they will or not. But my own course will be wholly uninfluenced by that of any one else. I have been cautioned by a great many people about attending this meeting to-night. I was told that it was an insidious attempt to disintegrate the democratic party, and a newspaper which joined us last fall, [laughter,] and my representative in Congress, who never joined us at all, have great fear that I will do something to disintegrate the democratic party. Now, if the whole party should differ with those to whom I have adverted, we should be no more disintegrated than we were before. My representative I have a very high opinion of. He seems to be very willing to represent the whole of our State and a very considerable part of New Jersey, [laughter;] and, looking at his paper this evening, I perceive that he has taken charge of the governments of Ohio, Indiana and Illinois, and several other States. It is not often that a man is found provided with such extensive plans of usefulness. I read a speech that he made before the Democratic Union Association on the 3d of March, as it was reported in the *World* on the 4th. Without undertaking to say what was proper for him to say or for him to omit, I will say that I thank God that he was not my representative until noon the next day. The democratic party, as you all know, nine years out of ten controls the government of the country. It requires, therefore, no great patriotism on their part to be attached to the government and the country. It is, in fact, an attachment to themselves. [Laughter.] As a general rule, they are wise, prudent and patriotic. Occasionally blind guides or bad drivers take some sleepy passengers into bad roads and upset them, as they did in 1848. [Laughter.] But then they wake up ; the passen_gers get out ; [laughter;] they inquire the right road ; they get a lantern, and examine the condition of affairs, and eventually they come all right. [Laughter.] I think they will do so now ; and yet it seemed to me, as a careful man, looking at their course just at this moment, that it was prudent for me to get out and walk. [Great laughter—"three cheers."] Whether I shall stop the coach to get in again or not, or foot it through, depends upon circumstances. [Renewed laughter.] But, fellow-citizens, whatever else I may do, whatever anybody else does, *I* shall sustain this war to the bitter end, [cheers,] and the city of New-York will do it. After sending eighty thousand men and spending three hundred millions of dollars, they will not hesitate to go through; and the State, in my humble judgment, will not hesitate to go through. Why, was there ever anything more preposterous than the idea that when we are told by the Southern men that we must recognize their independence before they will treat with us, that we should be wasting time in undertaking to negotiate a peace ? When the President of the Confederate republic, as he claims to be, denounced the best men of the North, and East, and West as pirates and hyenas, and, what he seems to suppose as worse than all, as Yankees, [laughter,] is it possible to make terms with him, or listen with composure to any arrangement for an accommodation?

["No."] Why, who are the men that have been sent from the State of New-York who are thus denounced by this rebel chieftain? I have differed from a great many of them politically—I have differed from a great many of them personally; but when you find the Kearnys, the Van Rensselaers, the Hamiltons, the Schuylers, the Dixes, the Kembles, the Jays, the Heckschers, the Cuttings, the Costers, the Cochrans, the Neills, the Emmets, the Cambrelings, the Duers, the Pratts, the Lydigs, the Kings, the Wadsworths, the Howlands, the Ulshoeffers, the Tompkins's and the Vosburghs, the best blood of the State of New-York, who are thus denounced as pirates, why, I submit that it requires more than ordinary composure to listen to it. Yankees! They are the Knickerbackers of New-York; they are the best men of the State of New-York; and when they peril their lives and shed their blood in defence of the Constitution of the country and the Union of the States, he who denounces them as pirates and hyenas is as forgetful of all the principles of truth and honor that should govern the language of a gentleman, as he is traitorous to the flag under which he acquired political fame. [Loud applause.]

We have nothing to do but fight this matter through. We can have no discretion in regard to it, and it behooves us to look around and see what assistance we are to receive, or what interference we are to meet with. Let me say one moment to you, that I am not one of those who unite in this sentiment of anxiety about the course of Great Britain. I happen to have had peculiar opportunities, which it is not necessary now to advert to, for knowing the people of Great Britain for the last thirty years. They will be neutral, and, in my humble judgment, that is all we have the right to expect. Nations are like individuals. When two gentlemen resort to the arbitrament of arms, no other person feels himself at liberty to interfere in the quarrel, and when two nations, cultivated and civilized, or claiming to be such, resort to arms, all we have a right to ask, in my humble judgment, of any third Power, is that they shall not interfere, but shall stand neutral. Now, all the public acts of the Government of Great Britain, all the declarations of her prominent men, all the correspondence of her Minister, all the general sources of information, compel us to believe that they mean to observe strict neutrality. Gentlemen tell me that they allow vessels to be fitted out at their private ship-yards. Well, it is for us to remember that we are to be at peace before long, and Europe is to be at war, and whatever our ship-yards or the owners of them, and our merchants say, they will allow the Government of the United States to forbid them from doing when European nations are at war, exactly that we have a right to insist that the British Government shall prohibit the ship-builders of Great Britain from doing. No more and no less. We must live up to our own law. Now, it is not a violation of any neutrality act, in my judgment, in subjects of Great Britain or citizens here, to build a ship and sell it to a government that is at war with them or us. It is seized as contraband, if you can get it—fair prize of war;

but it is no violation of the neutrality of Great Britain, and no violation of our neutrality. If our ship-owners and ship-builders desire such an amendment to be made to the neutrality act of Great Britain, then it is a fair matter of discussion whether it shall be done. But we cannot compel them to do any more than we are willing to do ourselves. But the Government and people of Great Britain have unquestionably a sympathy with the people of the Northern States in this contest, and while they do not feel at liberty to interfere, and ought not to be asked to interfere, in my humble judgment, we have their good wishes, and never need apprehend any acts on their part of an unfriendly character. Russia, beyond all doubt, is entirely friendly. The Emperor of the French will do exactly as he thinks is entirely for his own interest. I am not one of those who attach any importance to what he declares he will do, because his declarations to the French people were never kept, and I have no idea that his declaration to us will be observed unless it is for his benefit. He and his prominent men about him have nothing in their past lives to offer as hostages for their conduct. They live in the present. He holds his Government by force—whatever is necessary to maintain himself, that is exactly what he will do. And, in my judgment, when he sees that he must go on alone, that he will have no co-operation from other Powers, he will refuse to interfere in this quarrel, and will let us alone. But, gentlemen, we must depend upon ourselves. If we can fight this battle to victory, we shall be victorious—if we cannot, we shall be defeated. But beyond all earthly considerations we must unite—that is our highest obligation—and being united, I have no doubt about the result. I do not look forward to a long war—a great many people do. It is not the habit of modern times to have long wars. The great improvement in the engines of destruction and in means of communication enables nations to bring wars rapidly to a close. The Russian campaign was not long ; the Italian campaign was a short one, and in my judgment this war will be a short one if we are united and put forward the whole power of the loyal States of this Union. With our immense population and resources we ought to end this war in ninety days. Start your troops in New Orleans, at Vicksburg. at Charleston, and in Tennessee. Charge along the whole line—advance with energy and will—and my word for it, in ninety days everybody will wonder that this rebellion was ever regarded as formidable in any portion of the United States. [Prolonged cheers.]

The speech of Mr. Van Buren was received with marked attention, and his felicitous points were responded to with vociferous applause.

The Mayor then called upon the Hon. Henry J. Raymond.

G

## REMARKS OF MR. RAYMOND.

FELLOW-CITIZENS,—I should feel that it would be a most unwarrantable trespass upon your patriotic patience, already tried perhaps too long, were I to detain you by any remarks of my own at this late hour of the evening. I have come forward, at the request of gentlemen of the Committee, merely to read to you a letter from a distinguished citizen and servant of the Republic, which I am sure you will be glad to hear.

Mr. RAYMOND then read the following

*Letter from Mr. Secretary Seward.*

DEPARTMENT OF STATE, }
WASHINGTON, *March* 3, 1863. }

*To the Hon. George Opdyke, and others, New-York:*

GENTLEMEN : I thank you for your invitation to the meeting to be held on the 6th inst., designed to resolve itself into a Loyal League of Union citizens, and I deeply regret that public occupations here prevent my acceptance.

I pray that my name may be enrolled in that League. I would prefer that distinction to any honors that my fellow-citizens could bestow upon me. If the country lives, as I trust it will, let me be remembered among those who labored to save it. If Providence could disappoint the dearest hopes of mankind, let not my name be found among those who proved unfaithful.

I subscribe to your proposed resolutions in their exact letter, and in their right loyal and patriotic spirit. I would reserve nothing whatever from the sacrifice which may be required by the country. He that preferreth himself, his fame or his fortune, his friend, his father, his mother, his wife, his child, his party or his sect, his state or his section, above his country, is not worthy to be a citizen of the best and noblest country that God has ever suffered to come into existence.

No one of us ought to object when called upon to reaffirm his devotion to the Union, however unconditionally. I would cheerfully renew the obligations of fidelity to it every day and every hour, in every place, at home or abroad, as often as any citizen should question my loyalty, or as often as the renewal of the obligation on my part should seem likely to confirm and strengthen any other citizen in his patriotic resolution. The reaffirmation is wholesome for ourselves, even if it influence no one else.

I am, gentlemen, your obedient servant,

WILLIAM H. SEWARD.

Mr. RAYMOND asked permission to say in regard to this letter that no better response could be made to its sentiments than is afforded by the aspect and enthusiasm of this majestic assemblage of the unconditional loyalists of the city of New-York. It was a sight, he said, to gladden the eyes and rejoice the heart of every patriot ; for it shows that, in spite of all divisions of sentiment on minor points, in spite of all differences of political opinion and of partisan relations, deep down in the American heart lives an abiding love for the nation that will not let it perish, and that will resist to the death every attempt to accomplish its destruction. [Loud applause, and cheers.] I have listened, said Mr. R., with a degree of gratification which language cannot express, to the utterances and exhortations to loyalty and patriotism from gentlemen eminent in the councils of the democratic party. They confirm me in the belief I have always cherished, that when the final struggle came we should stand together to rescue the Union from the perils that hang over it—to subdue the rebellion—to hold aloft now and forever that glittering flag which is the ensign of our power and the emblem of freedom throughout the world. [Cheers.] I see in the proceedings of this meeting no symptom of discouragement—no signs of faltering in the great war we are compelled to wage. The gentleman who preceded me, (Mr. Van Buren,) said he did not anticipate a long war. However this may be, we are here to declare that whether it be long or short, whether it last one year, or two years, or three years—until courage and love of freedom die out of the American heart, until we have ceased to respect the devotion of our fathers, and to love the flag of our country—we shall not cease to prosecute this war against rebellion and for the preservation of the Union, to a successful issue. [Loud and prolonged applause.] For myself, I have had no misgivings as to the courage and purpose of the American people. I care not what party may have the guidance of the Government ; so far as the result is concerned I should have no fears of the issue if the Democratic party were to come into power to-morrow in every State and in the capital at Washington—the war could have but one result. It would still be carried forward to a successful issue. [Applause.] I say this, first, because I have the profoundest faith in the loyalty and fidelity of the American people ; and secondly, because no other result is possible. We must conquer the rebellion, or the rebellion must conquer us. [Applause.] No Democrat, no Republican, no Abolitionist, no Secessionist, no foreign power on earth can bring it to any other issue. [Loud applause.] And if any man believes that the American people will consent to see this nation destroyed and reduced to the condition of the republics of South America, so long as they have a dollar to spend or a blow to strike in its defence, his heart must either be faint with fear or tainted with disloyalty. [Applause.] It is not in the American heart to let this nation die. All minor issues will take care of themselves. The great question to be decided is not whether the writ of *habeas corpus* shall be suspended. nor whether freedom of speech shall be preserved, nor whether slavery shall be maintained or destroyed. The question is, Shall the *nation* live? [Loud cheers.] Settle that, and you settle all the rest. Secure the nation's life, and you secure the life of all those personal rights, those individual liberties, and that great principle of universal freedom which find their sole guarantee in the Constitution, and the only ability to maintain them in the flag of the Union and the power of which it is the emblem. [Cheers.] Let the nation live, and no power on earth can destroy the writ of *habeas corpus*, break down freedom of speech, or perpetuate human slavery on this continent. [Applause.] Let the nation die and no prophetic tongue can tell how soon the triumphant power of slavery will destroy every vestige of civil freedom in every part and on every foot of the continent. [Cheers.]

One word on another point. Reference has been made to the possibilities of foreign intervention. Whether such intervention will take place or not, is at present purely a matter of opinion. If it comes at all, I think it will come from the Emperor of France ; and in that event I believe it will bring with it more of advantage than of danger to the Union cause. I believe that its effect would be, first, to unite as one man the whole loyal population of the Northern States ; next, to alarm and arouse the great mass of the people of the South to the danger to which the restless and unprincipled ambition of Napoleon would expose them, and thus lead to the overthrow of the rebel Government ; and finally, to bring England to the side of the Union in the contest that would ensue. [Cheers.] And now, without entering upon any consideration of this important subject, believing that whatever we may think of it we shall all agree in claiming full and complete immunity from foreign interference, I beg leave to close my remarks by offering, as I do with the assent of the officers of the meeting, for your acceptance, the following resolution :—

*Resolved,* That we approve the action of the President and the Congress of the United States in declining—as unfriendly in its tendencies and effects—all intervention or mediation of foreign Powers, in any form or on any pretext, in the contest which the nation is compelled to wage for the perpetuation of its existence.

The resolution was unanimously adopted with loud applause.

Mr. WETMORE said :—I have now to submit to the meeting a letter from one of our most influential and patriotic citizens, Mr. A. T. STEWART, and, with the permission of the Chair, will read it :—

## MR. STEWART'S LETTER AND RESOLUTION.

BROADWAY, CORNER CHAMBERS-STREET, }
*March* 5, 1863. }

*Messrs. Geo. Opdyke and others, Committee :*

GENTLEMEN,—I gladly accept the honor of being an officer of the meeting to be held at the Cooper Institute to-morrow evening, to sustain the Government and the Union, and beg leave to suggest the following resolution, in addition to those proposed by the Committee :—

*Resolved,* That, in the judgment of this meeting, the resort of the Government to a currency of its own, for the purpose of meeting the extraordinary expenses caused by the rebellion, and made available for the payment of debts, public and private, was a necessity which could not have been avoided ; and that, as such currency binds all the property, real and personal, owned within the limits of the United States, it constitutes an obligation of unequalled authority and value, the upholding of which, by its ready acceptance, by inspiring confidence in its validity and safety, and by denouncing all efforts to discredit it, by whomsoever made or for whatever purpose, are duties as imperative as any now appertaining to an American citizen.

Yours, very truly,
ALEXANDER T. STEWART.

The Chairman put the question on the resolution, and it was unanimously adopted.

The Hon. D. K. CARTER, of Ohio, was then introduced.

## SPEECH OF HON. MR. CARTER.

The Hon. DAVID K. CARTER, of Ohio, was introduced, and said :—There is an accumulation of reasons why I should not address you at any length. In the first place, you have been patient listeners to long addresses from distinguished gentlemen, who have interested you better than I am capable of doing; another reason is, that the evening is exhausted ; and still a further reason is, that this is not the hour for talking; that hour has past, and the hour of action has come and is departing. [Cheers.] Let me say a word in a direction that the speeches you have listened to have not taken—a word of encouragement. Most of the speeches made at this time are marked with a tone of despondency. There is no occasion for it. I do not agree that this is to be a brief war, either. The great mistake in connection with it, from the time the rebellion was inaugurated to this hour, is, that the people have been taught impatience in the contest. It may be a long war ; and if it is to be fatal to the prosperity of the country, I hope it will be longer than my life. [Cheers.] But what is there in mapping out the progress made by our arms to-day that should lead us to despond ? The whole Mississippi Valley, with the exception of two points, is in our posses- sion. Missouri is redeemed ; Kentucky is redeemed ; Maryland is redeemed ; two-thirds of Tennessee is redeemed ; Louisiana is ours ; North Carolina is ours ; two-thirds of Virginia is in possession of the Federal arms ; the rebellion has been driven back into the heart of " intensified Niggerdom." [Cheers.] Why, the death-rattle has been heard in the throat of this rebellion for the last three months. They have stopped fighting this campaign beyond the lines, and they are merely staggering under a defensive movement, with short food and short clothing—and too much of that clothing sent from your city, smuggled into their lines. They are now fighting their battles in the North, and through two nations of Europe. [Applause.]

Now I wish to talk very considerately about England, very respectfully. I have a sort of notion that some of my ancestors may have come from there. [Laughter.] But my testimony to-night, and the testimony of history will be, when the events of this war are recorded, that British men, and British money, and British influence, have kept this rebellion alive. [Applause.] It is my solemn conviction at this hour, that Britain has fought this Republic in the most effectual way that her power permitted her to do. Hers are the privateers that prey upon our commerce, hers the guns that mount them, hers the ammunition and hers the tars that man them. Why, it ceases to be a secret ; they are openly dispatched from the ports of Britain. It is done under the guise of neutrality, and why ? Because an *open* war between Great Britain and the United States would let loose the privateers of America upon their commerce. [Cheers.] She can fight us in no other way. She made a show of it. She sent 40,000 men over here to

Canada, to make the pretence of war, perfectly ridiculous, when contrasted with the armies we are raising on this side of the Lake. [Applause.]

Why, this rebellion had not fairly burst out, it had not matured itself, it had not become an overt act, before Britain interfered to recognize them as belligerents of war. And why? Because her aristocracy looks upon the destruction of this Government as the saving condition of their hereditary institutions. [Cheers.]

The rebels are also fighting their battles in the North. They have their agents and officers in your midst. [A Voice.—"Fernando Wood and Booby Brooks!"] Ah! I wish you to speak of Brooks kindly. He was an old companion of mine in Congress. But "Booby" Brooks—if that is his name, [laughter,] he was called "James" when I knew him—is one of the rebels' agents in this city. And how is it, New-Yorkers—let me put this plain question to you in plain Western style—how is it that a sheet, teeming with treason from Monday to Saturday, and from the first of January to the last of December, is patronized in this heart of the Republic? Now, Brooks must make money out of it, some way or other; for nobody ever suspected him of having any principle, [cheers;] he must make by the distribution of his filthy sheet: and that distribution depends upon your patronage. And how is it, if (as I have always supposed, and as the gentlemen who preceded me have stated) you are loyal here, that this torch-light of treason is suffered to burn every evening in your city? [Cheers.] Now, this is a part of Jeff. Davis's army. He is fighting his battles more effectually by this means than by his poor devils of conscripts who are traveling barefooted in rebeldom. He is engaging your attention by side issues, in clamoring and fault-finding: and that is a characteristic of all fools, to be more ready to find fault than engage in the work in hand. [Cheers.] Be united, and this rebellion will perish before a united North. [Applause.] How soon I do not know; but God grant it may not be soon enough not to make a perfect cure! [Cheers.] Let us cut this ulcer from the root.

But I do not propose to make a speech. You have already listened long enough. [Cries of "Go on!"] Another mode of fighting this rebellion in these Free States, is to get up a clamorous contest about who shall be Justice of the Peace in Utica. [Laughter.] An outsider would suppose from the great hullabaloo made about the election in this State last fall, that the whole earth revolved about the single issue, and that the judgment-day was just behind it. [Cheers and laughter.] Now, do you not suppose that Jeff. Davis understands this fiddling, while Rome is burning? Does he not know perfectly well, while you are busy about the important matter of who shall be your Mayor or your Constable, that you are not reducing this rebellion and restoring the republic to its integrity again?

What would you think of a man who expected the Angel Gabriel to call for him to-morrow, and who would sit down to figure up the democratic majority in some township over a Constable's election? [Laughter.] And yet this great

State of New-York, and the great State of which I am proud to be a native. has been engaged in that sort of business ; and while we are thus engaged, Jeff. Davis has been laughing in his sleeve at our stupidity. I tell you that one of the happiest circumstances marking this contest and the desperation of Jeff. Davis of his conspiracy for the destruction of this country is, that he has been compelled to come down from his high estate, to treat us with indignity and insult. For Jeff. Davis has wisdom enough to know that he cannot commence making a bargain upon this subject without losing his army, that can never be rallied. He understands that "like a wild man!" [Laughter.] He has got to keep his forces up to the fighting line, under whip and spur.

My friend, Mr. Van Buren, has alluded to his calling us "hyenas." I wish to God it was true! [Cheers.] We have prosecuted this war more like sheep than hyenas. [Applause.]

I am thankful for the attention you have given me. I wished to declare my devotion to this cause. I went to South America, two years ago, the father of two grown-up sons. One lies in a soldier's grave ; the other is liable to lie there to-morrow ; and I would far sooner lie there myself than see this republic break up. [Applause.]

Three cheers were here given for Mr. Carter.

---

GENERAL WETMORE.—Allow me to call your attention to the fact that you have formed yourselves into a society to-night. Do not forget it. You will shortly be called together again, and let every man come. We will have something to interest you every time you come. [Cheers.] And now I have a motion to make:— That every gentleman who has spoken here to-night be elected by your voices an honorary member of the Loyal League of New-York.

The motion was carried by acclamation, and the meeting adjourned, giving three cheers for the Union, the Constitution, and the success of the war.

The following letters were read, being but exponents of a large number received by the Committee:—

## LETTER FROM HON. MONTGOMERY BLAIR, POSTMASTER-GENERAL.

WASHINGTON, 5th March, 1863.

*Messrs. Opdyke, and others:*

GENTLEMEN,—I regret that I cannot be with the loyal men of New-York to-morrow. I heartily approve the movement and the resolutions to be submitted at the meeting.

The lovers of the government should be thoroughly roused to a sense of the necessity of constant, united and vigorous efforts to preserve for mankind the happy progress of our Great Republic, which, in less than a century, has erected in the New World a nation blessed with a prosperity hitherto unknown. This prosperous power is the creation of popular government on a vast scale, and the struggle in which we are now involved a resistance to a most formidable conspiracy of oligarchs at home and abroad to destroy it.

It is not permanently to dismember its territory that this great government is now assailed. Its vital principle—popular sovereignty—is struck at. The physical conformation of our country defies all attempts to dissever the Union. Its lakes and Gulf—north and south—its rivers traversing east and west, from ranges of mountains, terminating in immense bays of the Atlantic and Pacific, and vast navigable streams in the central valleys, which are channels of commerce, bringing the seas to the homes of all the cultivators of the continent, renders the dissolution of the Union which grows out of the necessities of commerce as impossible as the destruction of the system provided by nature for that intercourse. England and Scotland are not more marked as the home of one people and one government than our country. Perpetual, unmitigated hostility was the fate of the English and Scotch people until they became one under the same government, and so it would be of us.

But whilst the conspiracy against the government cannot permanently dismember a Union born of natural causes and bounded by natural limits, it may, and will, if successful, change the character of that government by blotting out the free principles inscribed in our *Magna Charta* at its birth, and adopting the counter-declaration of the rebellion, which makes *Slavery* the foundation of the new institution to give law to the continent. The prophetic heart of the President long ago foretold the issue which the Southern agitators were forcing on the country, when he said, in one of his early contests for freedom, " I see that the United States must all be Free or all Slave," and this is the issue of the hour — not of debate, but of arms. We must conquer, or the irresistible power of the Union itself will subject us to the oligarchs.

I am, very respectfully,

Your obedient servant,

[Signed.]                                    M. BLAIR.

## LETTER FROM MAJOR-GENERAL BURNSIDE.

WASHINGTON, *Friday, March 6th*, 1863.

*To George Opdyke. Jonathan Sturges, and others, Committee:*

GENTLEMEN,—I regret that my public duties will prevent my acceptance of your kind invitation to be present at a meeting of loyal citizens of New-York, at the Cooper Institute, this evening. The resolutions which it is proposed to introduce are in exact accordance with my sentiments. It is clearly the duty of every " citizen, sailor and soldier " to give to the government his unconditional and most effective support. A conditional support is full of discord, danger and disaster, and at a time like the present, amounts to disloyalty. In view of all the resources with which God has blessed us, it would be ignominious to believe that we have not the physical ability to maintain the government, when we remember that we are fighting to sustain a government that originated in truth, justice, honor and patriotism, against a rebellion that originated in deceit, fraud, ambition and ignorance. It would be distrusting God's justice to believe that final success will not attend our efforts.

If we see evils before us, let us do all in our power to correct them in a temperate way. Our legislators should be made to feel that they misrepresent us when they attempt to clog the wheels of government, or indulge in party legislation.

Politics and party lines should be ignored for the present. Fraudulent contractors and dishonest disbursing officers should be punished. Officers and soldiers should be subordinate, patriotic, energetic and free from all personal ambition. The law of Congress making every man a soldier who is capable of bearing arms should be enforced and submitted to. The old regiments should be kept full, and promotions made from soldiers and officers in the field, for merit.

The President and Governors should be always surrounded by honest, loyal and patriotic men, capable of giving advice in their several departments. The Press should be temperate and independent; and, finally, our whole people— men, women and children—should be loyal, patriotic and honest, trusting in the righteousness of our cause, and cheerfully submitting to all the privations which the Providence of God may visit upon us. Who will believe that this rebellion could last another year if we were all resolved to fulfill these conditions?

Thanking you, gentlemen, for the high honor done me by this kind invitation,

I remain, very respectfully,

Your obedient servant,

A. E. BURNSIDE, *Major-General.*

---

## REPLY FROM BRIG.-GENERAL BARNARD.

WASHINGTON, *March* 11, 1863.

*Messrs. George Opdyke, Jonathan Sturges, and others:*

GENTLEMEN,—I regret that my official avocations prevented my accepting your invitation to attend the "meeting of loyal citizens."

No one has felt more keenly the division of sentiment amongst ourselves, which has vented itself in mutual recriminations, and which, at one time, seemed to me to bid fair to paralyze the arm of our own national strength, at a moment when all that strength was most necessary.

This is no place to introduce topics of political controversy, but when "loyal citizens" appeal to their fellow-citizens to unite in sustaining a righteous war, all must be conscious that there is but *one* Constitutional rallying point.

All patriotic men should be able to say with Governor Todd, " I support Mr. Lincoln, not because he is a Republican, not because he is a tariff man or an antislavery man, but because he is President of the United States, and, by virtue of his office, entitled to the support of all loyal men."

When it is the admitted duty of patriotic men thus to feel and thus to act, it would be sad, indeed, if the Administration represented by Mr. Lincoln, around

## LETTER FROM DR. FRANCIS LIEBER.

NEW-YORK, *Thursday, March 5, 1863.*

MY DEAR SIR :

Most heartily and fervently do I approve of the resolutions sent me, and feel honored that I am to serve as an officer of the meeting.
But Cooper Institute is too small—at least I hope so.

Very truly, yours,

FRANCIS LIEBER.

Hon. GEORGE OPDYKE, &c., New-York.

---

## LETTER FROM W. H. WEBB.

NEW-YORK, *March 4, 1863.*

*Hon. George Opdyke, and others :*

GENTLEMEN,—I most heartily approve of the proposal to convene a public meeting of loyal citizens, and also of the resolutions to be submitted to the meeting, and am ready to co-operate in any effort to this end.

Yours, respectfully,

W. H. WEBB.

---

## LETTER FROM JOHN AUSTIN STEVENS, JR.

CHAMBER OF COMMERCE OF THE STATE OF NEW-YORK, }
NEW-YORK, *March 5th,* 1863. {

SIR :

I will cheerfully act as one of the officers of the meeting called for to-morrow evening at the Cooper Institute.
I think it quite time that our noble city repudiated all sympathy with treason, and placed her mark on the copperhead.

Respectfully,

JOHN AUSTIN STEVENS, JR.

To the MANAGER, P. O. Box 610.

---

## LETTER FROM LEONARD W. JEROME.

*March 5, 1863.*

GENTLEMEN :

I accept with pleasure your polite invitation, and beg you to designate me for any office of the meeting you please, from a Vice-President to a lamplighter.
I shall be there and serve.

With great respect,

LEONARD W. JEROME.

Messrs. OPDYKE and others.

# OUTSIDE MEETINGS.

Owing to the immense mass of citizens who assembled at the place of meeting, thousands who were unable to obtain standing room in the great Hall, had to remain outside, crowding the large balconies, front and rear, surrounding the entire building, and filling the adjacent squares.

Several open-air meetings were improvised, and stirring speeches were made by Hon. James Wadsworth, Colonel James Fairman, J. C. Anderson, and a number of other gentlemen.

The whole surrounding space was brilliantly illuminated by calcium lights, which added greatly to the effect of the interesting occasion.

A band of music had been provided for the emergency, and spirit-stirring, patriotic strains enlivened the scene and kept the vast concourse in rapt enjoyment until midnight.

It will be long before this noble ovation to loyal principles and loyal duty will be forgotten by the Union-loving people of New-York.

www.ingramcontent.com/pod-product-compliance
Lightning Source LLC
Chambersburg PA
CBHW030904260626
47169CB00008B/2683

* 9 7 8 3 3 3 7 3 6 7 8 2 4 *